BROKEN
hearts

even broken hearts can love again...

www.chellebliss.com

CHELLE BLISS
USA TODAY BESTSELLING AUTHOR

thank you for buying the print edition

Download the eBook version for FREE!

Scan the QR code below, add the eBook to your cart, and
the 100% discount will be shown at checkout.

the eBook will be instantly delivered to your email via Bookfunnel

BROKEN HEARTS © 2025

———

Publisher © Bliss Ink January 14th 2025
Edited by Lisa A. Hollett
Proofread by Read By Rose & Shelley Charlton
Cover Design © Chelle Bliss
Cover Photo © FuriousFotog
Cover Model Alex Pomeroy

Chelle Bliss
MENOFINKBB.COM

OPEN ROAD SERIES

Book 1 - Broken Sparrow (Morris)
Book 2 - Broken Dove (Leo)
Book 3 - Broken Wings (Crow)
Book 4 - Broken Arrow (Arrow)
Book 5 - Broken Hearts (Eagle)

The Open Road series is interconnected with the Men of Inked: Heatwave series. Learn more at menofinked. com/heatwave-series

Also available in alternative paperback editions

CHAPTER 1
LACEY

DO NOT *lust after the biker*.

Do not lust after the biker.

And once more, because I know that today, of all days, my brain is not listening: *Do not lust after the biker*.

I repeat the phrase in my head over and over in time with the click of my high heels as I head into Villa Lantana. I work at South Florida's most exclusive event destination, and coming to work here is normally the best part of my day. I love what I do, and—the cherry on top—I love where I get to do it.

Today, my stomach is clenching with anxiety. The events on the schedule this weekend—not just one night, but the whole damn weekend—are going to force me to look one of my worst mistakes right in the eye. And of course, I have to do it with a *smile*. Because even though my ex is a dirtbag, I'm the director of events. Living my dream working weddings, corporate events, parties. Planning every little detail, organizing, and making sure our guests are blissfully happy. But this weekend, I'm going to be one miserable woman—even if I have to eat a shit sandwich with a smile on my face.

I sigh as I stride past a stunning concrete fountain, the tinkling sound of falling water soothing my heart even though my nerves are particularly frazzled.

The Florida humidity is nearly melting my makeup off, so I hurry to pull open the aged brass door handle, grateful for the blast of chilly air that greets me as the glass door opens and I step inside the lobby.

The lobby walls are covered with elegant wallpaper that's green and gold with lovely pink blooms that highlight the pink marble floors. Large mirrors in massive gold frames ordinarily make me smile, but today, all I see is my sour expression reflected back at me.

I straighten my shoulders and remind myself that no matter how hard this weekend will be, no matter how hard the meeting I have this morning will be, I've got this.

I just have to convince the bikers to help me.

"Quiet morning, Bob?" I ask, smiling at the older man behind the front desk as I pass.

"My favorite kind, Ms. Mercer," he says with a nod.

I smooth back the loose strands that have slipped out of my bun and hustle down the pink marble corridor that leads to my office. Balancing my massive bag over my shoulder, I unlock my door, thrilled to find that my assistant remembered to program my coffeemaker before she left last night.

Do not lust after the biker, I repeat as I watch the pot brew. The dreamy aroma of fresh, strong coffee immediately releases the tension in my shoulders.

As soon as I pour a cup, I fire up my laptop and check my email, scolding myself for having yet another foolish crush on a man who can't be any good for me.

Eagle.

He's a biker, member of a local motorcycle club—not gang, as I was quickly corrected the first time I said it.

I had no experience with motorcycle clubs until Eagle and his brother from the club, Brute. I hired them two years ago to work security after one of the guys from the private security company we had been using failed to stop a fight between a brokenhearted groomsman and a groom. That was a serious PR nightmare for the Lantana, and I learned then that our event security needed to be ready to actually provide security. We needed a lot more than sweet old men in uniforms who were more interested in free dinners than keeping order and playing bouncer.

I tried hiring a few security firms, but that did not go well. There are a lot of legal issues when it comes to bringing on contract security, and while I absolutely follow the letter of the law in everything I do, I didn't really feel safe with any of the firms I interviewed. That's sort of ironic when you consider that I ended up feeling safe around the meanest-looking bikers I could find.

And that's how I met him.

Eagle.

He has a real name, of course. It's on his employment paperwork, but ever since he extended a heavily tattooed hand to shake mine and told me to call him Eagle, that's who he's been to me.

That, and the object of a lot of incredibly intense and hot fantasies lately.

Eagle.

Just thinking his name makes my body quiver and a little sweat break out along my hairline.

I don't understand why I have this crush on him. He's no Ken doll, that's for damned sure. But the last few guys I've met have had the looks and the bodies to rival a Ken, and yet they were total shits.

Maybe I've been going after the wrong types all these years. Maybe giving in to lusting after my biker employee is just the thing to renew my faith in men.

I shake my head to get the foolish thoughts moving. Romance and love are just that—foolish. I see couples every single day who are supposed to love each other through thick and thin, and yet they fight, bicker, and betray each other.

I've been the fighter, the bicker-er, and oh, how I've been betrayed by guys I thought loved me. I should be done with romance. Should be over girlish dreams. Especially after my experience with the asshole ex I'm going to have to see this weekend.

Speaking of the asshole ex... He won't just be attending the wedding I'm managing this weekend. But Dirtbag Dylan is the freaking father of the bride, who's still married to the mother of the bride.

Was he always married? Yes, he was. Did he lie to me about being married during every single one of the fourteen months we dated? He did. And it wasn't just a basic lie he told me. It was massive.

I thought he was a widower.

I thought his wife was *dead*.

Turns out being dead and spending a couple of months at a med spa in Turkey mean the same thing to some people. Of course, he tried to tell me that he "thought" his wife was going to die. She went abroad to try some experimental treatment that she couldn't get here in the States. But then I met her when the whole family—both the bride's side and the groom's—came for a final walkthrough of the property.

That was when I discovered that the experimental treatment his poor, ailing wife got in Turkey was not experimental at all. It was just far cheaper to get a facelift and neck lift there than here in the States. And a far more discreet way to get a whole lotta work done before their daughter's wedding than having her show up with black eyes and bandages at the country club.

I ended things immediately when I found out that, no, his wife wasn't dead, and holy shit, she's hotter than a Barbie doll, although probably more plastic. But there was nothing I could do about the wedding.

The bride booked the venue more than a year before I met her father. And somehow, she has beaten the odds and is actually getting married to her fiancé, so now I have to sit through one whole weekend of events where the man who stomped on my heart walks his daughter down the aisle with his very much alive wife on his arm.

Yay, me.

I fill a second mug of coffee two-thirds of the way, stir in a touch of sugar, and splash a bit of milk from my mini fridge under the coffee bar. Then, holding my mug carefully so I don't spill a precious drop, I walk to the clothing rack hanging in the corner of my office.

I am never, ever going to get Eagle to agree to this. But I have to. He's simply got to do this. I can't find new security on short notice, and this change in our process is something Dirtbag Dylan's Botox Barbie wife just sprung on me last week.

Even through the transparent garment bag, I can see the designer tuxedo is luxurious. The fabric looks so dense and smooth, I want to run my hands down the midnight-blue panels. A bloom of heat threatens to break my entire body into a sweat. *Damn it.* This is exactly the reaction I did not want.

But who could blame me? The suit isn't just beautiful; it's massive. It has to be to fit Eagle's muscular shoulders. I imagine him, tuxedo jacket open, a slim matching tie loose around the collar of a crisp white shirt that hides all his tattoos except for the ones on the backs of his hands. It's gorgeous. He's gorgeous. And even for someone who's too heartbroken to date, Eagle is quite simply a walking wet dream.

Sweet mother.

I'm failing dismally at my efforts to stay cool. Picturing Eagle unbuttoning the cuffs, loosening his tie, moving the sumptuous fabric away from his colorful skin to give me a closer look…

"Not today, Satan," I remind myself. "Not any day, in fact."

I shake my head at my stupidity.

Still, I can't stop the naughty thoughts that make my skin tingle.

"Pull it together," I remind myself. "You're a professional."

"Pull what together?"

Flutters of electricity quiver along my nerve endings.

Shit. Fuck. Crap.

He's *here*. He's *early*.

I take a second to compose my expression, take a sip of coffee to fortify myself, and then slowly turn on my five-inch heels to face Eagle.

"You're early." I nod, all serious and professional, as though I don't feel like my entire body has melted an inch into my shoes at the sound of his voice. "Thanks for coming in."

The man filling the doorway of my office has shoulders so broad he fills up the entire width of the space. He's wearing a dark gray T-shirt that looks like it's painted over his sculpted chest and arms. The distressed black leather vest he wears over his tee has his biker name embroidered on a patch over his heart.

I suck in my lower lip as I take in thick biceps covered in colorful tattoos when he lifts an arm and leans it against the doorjamb. He tugs dark aviators from his eyes with a heavily tattooed hand and looks me over.

"Mornin', boss..." His voice is low and a little raspy. A bedroom voice. The voice of a man who can bring chills to a woman's skin just by whispering in her ear.

His eyes, bright blue like the Florida sky on the most perfect day, seem to study my lips, waiting for me to find my words.

I clear my throat, feeling every bit as awkward as I probably look, and walk back to my desk, putting a little too much swagger in my step in my hurry to get as much of the solid cherrywood between him and me as possible. Then I set down my mug and motion for him to come in.

"Have a seat," I say, my voice trembling slightly. I give my head a little shake, frowning and desperately hoping to clear my muddled thoughts.

Do not lust after the biker.

I'm going to have to treat myself to a new vibrator after this weekend. I'm going to need a hell of a release to manage the pent-up desire I feel for this man. After a whole weekend? And if I can get him to do what I need him to do? I'll be an embarrassing puddle of need before the bride even tosses the bouquet.

Eagle's still a good ten feet away from me, yet I swear, as I pull in a breath through my nose, a subtle whiff of aftershave and soap reaches my nose. I take in as much of the heavenly scent as I can before I realize he can probably tell what I'm doing.

As he approaches, the thick, well-worn soles of his boots scuff lightly against the floor. His stride is long, his legs looking muscular even through the faded denim of his well-worn jeans. I watch him a little too intently until he stops in front of my desk and lifts his brows.

"Something wrong?" I ask.

He looks down at the pristine silver fabric of the guest chair in front of my desk like he's afraid he's going to dirty it or break it. He mutters something low in his throat but drops into the chair and looks helplessly down at the armrests.

He's so big, he has to wedge himself into the seat. A lost expression, like he doesn't quite know what to do with his hands, comes over his face. His legs are spread wide, and he finally decides to rest his hands on his knees.

I've been watching him this entire time like a hormone-soaked teenager with a crush, and I immediately scold myself for being a weirdo. I'm his boss, for God's sake. And men suck. Love sucks. I need to pull myself together and get down to business. I snap my eyes to my laptop and start tapping at the keys just for something to do.

"So, what's up? Am I fired?" Eagle asks.

His pale skin is dusted with freckles and fine lines, weathered from years riding in the wind and sun. His hands are muscled like they've seen years of hard work. The silver threaded through his reddish hair and brows makes him look like a man who would chop down trees for fun.

I chuckle, a little too loudly, and answer his question. "Wait. What? Fired? Oh God, no. Why would you think that?"

He motions around with a tattooed hand. "Been working security for these fancy parties of yours for, what now…two years? I think this is the first time I've been called to the boss lady's office. Leads me to prepare for the worst. Unless you're here to offer me a fat raise, in which case, I accept."

I laugh at his joke about the raise, but then I swallow, thankful for the reminder. He's right. That's what I am. I'm the boss lady. His boss.

All the more reason why I can*not* lust after the biker.

Even if I can hardly help myself.

I force a smile, grateful he can't read my thoughts. "Eagle, no," I tell him. "God, no. You're not in trouble. Not at all. And I'm sorry, but I don't have a raise for you. Though, I do have some news. We have a special request for the wedding this weekend. The bride and groom have arranged some formalwear for you."

At that, a slow smile lifts one corner of his mouth. "Formalwear." He repeats the word, his eyes sparkling like he's about to burst out laughing.

"Yes, a tuxedo," I explain. "The bride and groom have covered the cost. We just need to fit you so you're comfortable at the event."

"A tuxedo?" He says the word low in his throat, and I find myself swallowing hard at the deep rasp.

God, how he can make saying a word like tuxedo sound erotic, I'll never know.

"Sorry, doll." Eagle shakes his head slowly. "Tux and comfortable don't fit in the same sentence. There ain't no way you're getting one of those things on my body." He stands to leave, pushing himself out of the tiny formal chair opposite my desk.

I knew he would take some convincing, but I wasn't prepared for this.

"Eagle, wait. You're leaving? Are you serious?" I rush to my feet.

He must be serious because he's halfway to the door before I realize I have to stop him.

I scurry around my desk and run as fast as my heels will allow across the marble. "Eagle, wait. Please. I need you at this wedding."

His back is to me, and I reach for his arm to stop him. My fingers are only resting on the bare skin of his bicep, but my traitorous bitch of a body tells me to hold on much tighter than is necessary.

His skin is so smooth and hot. I don't know what I expected him to feel like, but this is the first time I've touched him since I shook his hand when I hired him. I know, because I've been so, so careful not to touch him for this exact reason.

He looks down at my hand, and I yank it back, feeling horrible that I've crossed a line. He's my employee and I didn't do anything, but still. I take a fast step back just as Eagle turns to look down at me.

"Um, excuse me. Is Lacey there?" I hear a familiar voice calling past the mountain of man blocking her view of me. "You ready for the fitting?"

I clasp my hands together so I'm not tempted to do any more unauthorized touching. "Margaret," I call out. "Yes, please. Come on in."

Eagle steps aside to let the tailor I've hired past him. He crosses his arms over his chest and peers down at me. "I was just leaving," he reminds me, lifting his chin slightly.

"Eagle, please," I say. Hell, at this point, I'd drop to

my knees and beg. That's all I'd do—*beg*—if that meant I could get Eagle to work this weekend. But if he's going to work this wedding, I've got to get him to wear the tux.

"Eagle, meet Margaret, the tailor," I tell him. Then, without thinking, I blurt out, "Please, come back into my office. I need to get you out of your clothes."

CHAPTER 2
EAGLE

I WOULD TAKE off my clothes for this woman any day of the week, but if either one of us is going to strip down to what the good Lord gave us, I'd prefer to see *her* without that gray pencil skirt and white blouse. And I damn well want to be the one taking them off her piece by piece.

As soon as she says the words, my boss gasps like she can't believe what she just said and shakes her head. Her cheeks flush a deep red, and a rush of blood floods my cock.

Lacey is damned near the sexiest thing I've ever seen, but fuck, is she wound tight. What I wouldn't give to strip off her clothes and, with them, every single one of her inhibitions. And I'd start with that tight little knot of a bun at the back of her head. I'd love to know if she's a woman who likes a fistful of hair in her man's hand as he plows her from behind.

But those are exactly the kinds of thoughts that make me feel like I'm teetering on the edge at this job. I may not be fired today, but it's going to happen. Because this thing I've had for my boss for far too long is gonna take over someday. And when I put my big fucking boot in my mouth and say something I shouldn't—or, worse, take what I've always wanted to be mine—well, I know what will happen then. Pretty little Lacey Mercer's gonna walk my ass down the hall to HR and make sure the door hits me hard on my way out.

She's one woman who'd be worth losing the gig for, though. I'll tell you that much.

Even when she looks horrified, I can't stop my body from craving her. The bright-red lipstick highlights her lips forming a perfect O. Well, not a perfect O. That's what I'd give her if she gave me so much as half a chance to take her there. But fuck, she is sweet, flushing and looking flustered, when the truth is, I'd like her even more if she talked like that all the time. But I get it. Time and place. And this Margaret lady is a bit of a cockblock, so I have to let Lacey's comment go. For now.

And since I'm not fired, I jerk a thumb at the woman in practical flats who's got a tape measure around her neck and a little bag of what I assume are pins and scissors or some shit.

"Sorry to inconvenience you," I say. "Much as I'd love to strip down to my birthday suit, it ain't happening." I shake my head. "At least, not like this. I draw the line at the suit."

I give the wedding planner a look that'd make my worst enemy soil his shorts. But this lady ain't shaken.

Lacey meets my stare with a desperate, helpless expression that almost has me reconsidering my feelings about tuxedos.

"Eagle." I hear a little plea in her voice when she says my name, and the zipper of my jeans feels way too fucking tight around my cock. "Please?" she asks.

I slam my mouth shut before I say some shit I cannot take back. I'm like putty in this woman's hands, and I don't fucking like the feeling of falling into dangerous territory where I lose all control. But that's the type of woman Lacey Mercer is.

And that means Lacey Mercer is not my type.

Ah fuck, forget that. She's every man's type. Every man with eyes, at least.

What I should say is she's way, way out of my league. I couldn't dream of a woman like this wanting a bastard like me, and I don't know that I'd be enough for her even if she wanted me.

She's tall but wears sky-high heels that show off bare legs that I'd love to see wrapped around my shoulders. The tight bun at the nape of her neck gives off a sexy librarian vibe. And Lacey's eyes were made for fucking. I can't count the number of times I've imagined those eyes staring up at me while her lips wrap around my cock.

The tight skirts she wears can't hide her generous ass, an ass I want in my hands, on my face, bouncing on my lap. I've strained my vision so many times trying to peek at her tits behind those boring-ass blouses, I'm surprised I don't need glasses.

She turns that chocolate gaze on me and crosses her

arms over the nearly sheer white blouse, which only makes me that much more aware of the hell of a nice rack she's got buttoned down under the gauzy fabric.

"Eagle…" When my name slips from between her full red lips again, my blood heats, and I have to think about grandmas and other dick-softening images.

Thankfully, a second later, there's a whoop at the door, and a familiar voice breaks the tension and melts my hard-on with just two words. "Hey, asshole."

I hear the heavy stomp of boots, and then my brother's meaty fist punches me in the ribs.

Lacey gives us a stare, then lets out a sigh and looks from me to my brother from the club.

"Brute, good morning. Thank you for coming." Her voice is composed, bordering on cold, after how heated she was asking me to take off my clothes. I immediately miss the sound of her almost begging my name, even if she was only talking about work. She motions toward the tailor lady and then back to us. "Gentlemen," she says formally, a term that always makes me want to bust a nut laughing.

We aren't gentlemen. We're bikers—or, I guess, we were. Since the MC's gone clean, we do a lot less drinkin', fightin', and fuckin' than I'd like.

I miss the old days.

The days before Morris got himself an old lady and became a dad two times over. Before our club president found out he had a grown daughter and welcomed in a whole new generation of his family and became a fucking granddaddy.

These days, the Disciples are basically a social club

—nothing like what we used to be. But even thinking about it, I'm living in the past. A dream dead and buried. But the Disciples are still my family. My life.

All of my brothers have gone mostly legit. I'm the one who still hasn't found my footing. Maybe it's my age—more likely, it's my attitude—but this old dog ain't about new tricks. Working security at posh events is a far cry from busting heads in bars for fun, but I do get to threaten rowdy rich dickheads every once in a while. I get paid a shit-ton more than I can believe for standing around looking mean, which I don't even have to try to do. Sometimes the venue or the happy couple tosses in a meal and drinks on top of the pay. Not a bad gig for a motherfucker with no special skills except riding and making trouble.

Brute barks a laugh at the word gentlemen, but then he flicks a serious look at Lacey, as if just now it's hitting him that we've been summoned into our boss's office for a meeting three days before we're actually supposed to work an event. "What's this all about? We in some kind of trouble?" He shrugs. "What'd we do?"

"I already asked." I shrug back. "Appears not."

"Damn," Brute mutters, "I wouldn't mind a little trouble." He cracks his knuckles loudly, and I am about to start laughing when I see the tense look on Lacey's face.

"Go on, then," I say, meeting Lacey's eyes. "You convince Brute, and you got me too."

"Convince me of what?" Brute looks at the seam-stress lady, then frowns. "What'd I miss?"

I point to the clothing rack that has several garment

bags hanging on it. "We're about to get the Cinderella special," I tell him.

He looks confused, and just as he opens his mouth to curse somebody out, Lacey sighs.

"The wedding this weekend," she says, her voice catching just enough that I notice it. "The bride and groom have requested that even our security staff wear formalwear." She puts on a bright smile that doesn't reach her eyes and waves at the Margaret woman. "They've covered the costs. We just need to get you fitted. For your tuxedos."

Brute turns and heads back the way he came. "Nope. Not me. I'm out."

I turn to leave with him, but one look back at the slight tremble of Lacey's lower lip, and I stop dead. She doesn't look like she's about to cry; she looks vulnerable. Like if she says what's really on her mind, her careful mask will melt like an ice sculpture left out in the Florida sun.

"Yo, asshole. Hold up a sec." I nod at Brute, then turn back to Lacey. "Why the uniform now? Why this event?"

Brute and I have worked dozens of these events. Weddings, bar mitzvahs, reunions, holiday parties. Villa Lantana is an exclusive, expensive place. The kind of place you don't want to wipe your mouth on the napkins 'cause they're white silk or some shit.

I go more for the neon beer sign, varnished tables, and sticky floor vibe. But the gardens are beautiful, and they have a massive man-made pond with koi and swans that they fix up for fancy parties. Apparently, their insurance requires on-site security staff to make sure no one gets too drunk and takes a dunk. It hasn't been a problem so far, but I've helped plenty of old ladies out of their chairs over the last couple years. There's absolutely nothing about this job I can't do while wearing a decent suit. A tux seems like overkill, some overprivileged bride's wet dream.

"Isn't it some kind of safety risk to have us all dolled up?" I ask. "What if I gotta beat a guy down? That thing got any give to it?"

Margaret's the one who answers, her face going pale. She's unzipped one of the garment bags and is pulling a jacket from the hanger, inspecting the label. "These are Tom Ford," she explains, as if that should mean something. "These are easily five-thousand-dollar tuxedos. You're not going to get them bloody, are you?"

"Six," Lacey corrects softly. "They are six-thousand-dollar tuxedos. Each."

Brute whoops and slaps a hand against the shredded knee of his black jeans. "You're fucking with me," he says. "My first bike didn't cost six Gs."

I shoot Brute a look, growing more suspicious as the seconds pass. I'm used to the champagne crowd passing me a couple crisp hundreds in an envelope after a wedding—not a bad tip on top of my fixed rate for the easiest gig on the planet. But a uniform worth six grand?

I lift my chin. "What's the deal with the party?" I ask. "The bride a celeb?"

Lacey shakes her head. "No, no celebs. Nothing like

that. Just a wealthy couple whose parents want a certain experience for their kids' special day."

"Experience," Brute scoffs, and he looks like he's about to say something that would be better not to repeat in front of the woman who signs our checks, so I shoot him a look.

"You can keep them," Lacey says quickly, lifting her chin excitedly as if that is some kind of solution. "I know you may not have a lot of use for tuxedos, but they're not rented, so you can keep them after the event. Sell them, make a little cash back. I don't care what you do with them. But I need you to wear them." She looks at Brute, then me, her perfectly bowed lips pursed in thought. She meets my eyes, and for a second, she almost looks shy. The dip between her curved eyebrows upends me. "Please," she says. "I'd consider it a personal favor. Just this once."

The way she says please tugs at something deep in my chest, not to mention my groin. I heave a tired sigh. If I'm gonna be wrapped around anyone's little finger, I might as well do it dolled up in shit that cost more than an honest man should ever pay for freaking *clothes*.

"It's only for this wedding?" I clarify. "This ain't no regular thing?"

She visibly relaxes, as if she knows she's got me halfway there. She rushes to reassure me. "Yes, just this wedding, just this once. And as always, you can wear whatever you want to the rehearsal dinner and the Sunday brunch." She lifts a brow at Brute. "As long as it complies with the dress code," she adds, making sure

Brute knows his frayed band tees and leathers are never going to be appropriate attire at the Lantana.

I sigh, knowing full well I'm done for. Lacey wants this. Lacey sounds like she needs this. And since I both want and need my boss in ways that I don't want to think too hard about, I know I'm gonna cave. I may be a fucking pussy, but at least I'll be a pussy in a six-grand designer suit.

I nod at Brute. "You in?" I ask, making it clear from my tone that we're in.

He cocks his head and chuckles. "Aw, why the fuck not. I ain't worn a tux since junior prom. Maybe I'll get lucky wearing it this time."

I laugh, doubting that Brute needs a Tom Ford suit to get laid, and I shrug out of my leather vest. I make sure my eyes meet Lacey's as I ask, "So, where do we get naked?"

CHAPTER 3
LACEY

I ARRIVE at the rehearsal dinner in a formfitting little black dress with spaghetti straps. My nerves are so frayed, my skin is itching. I normally would dress a little less sexy, a little more professional, but I'm on fumes over here. I need every tool I've got to feel powerful, together, and hot enough to pound the heart out of the father of the bride if I need to.

Fuck his Barbie wife.

Fuck his lies.

I went all in for tonight, and I don't regret my choice of spike heels. At least…not yet.

The bride and groom aren't due to arrive for another hour, but since the entire family is staying on the Lantana estate for the weekend, various elderly aunts and uncles arrive early to the dining space.

My hospitality staff of eighteen is already in place. The tables are extravagantly set with bright yellow and orange flowers, pale yellow water goblets, and lots of vibrant fresh greens. Perfectly caramelized Portuguese egg custard tarts are displayed on tall, tiered crystal cake displays beside petit fours wrapped in pale yellow mini cupcake papers, our chef's elegant take on the Welsh tea cake. These touches, the menu that honors both sides of the family's heritage, are just part of what makes the Lantana so special.

If I weren't dreading everything about this wedding, I'd feel the same pride I always do at the beautiful work we do. But tonight, the only thing I can feel is dread. Well, that, and some simmering resentment, plus a side portion of good old-fashioned rage. I cannot believe I have to see the man who lied to my face while holding my body, loving me in every way I thought a man could, and doing it for months. And because I value my job more than just about anything in my life, I couldn't quit when I found out that the man I'd been fucked over by would be walking his little girl down our aisle.

Even though I ended things with Dylan months ago, I still can't help beating myself up for being too stupid to see the truth. I mean, weren't there signs? Aren't there always with married men?

I really should have known. I really should have trusted less and verified more. Dylan Acosta was a filthy, filthy liar, but me? I was starry-eyed and stupid, through and through. Me and my Ken doll dreams, be damned. And now, I just have to get through this weekend. If I can do that, I will never, ever have to see Dirtbag Dylan again.

I suck in a breath and suck in my gut, telling myself

I can manage my emotions. With any luck, Dylan will be so consumed with his very much alive and breathing wife, his daughter, and his soon-to-be son-in-law, he will barely even notice I'm here.

If I'm really lucky, he might even pretend not to know me. Which is exactly what a man with half a brain and even a sliver of conscience would do.

I survey the activity from the far corner of the room, where an elegant white marble bar is lit by soft Edison bulbs and string lights. My hair is loose tonight, the collarbone-length cut razor-sharp and smooth. I peek at my blood-red lipstick in the mirror behind the bar until the bartenders hustle in carrying trays of condiments and interrupt my view.

I adjust the tiny earpiece and receiver clipped to my dress and click the button to answer a question from the head of housekeeping through a discreet walkie-talkie. The last hour before the event begins is basically controlled chaos, with me troubleshooting everything from a clogged toilet in the men's room to a missing picture frame that the couple wants the wedding party to sign.

By the time the villa fills with guests, I'm already exhausted, and the night hasn't even begun.

As I stand near the bar, keeping watch on the servers, how the guests are responding to the food, and generally monitoring my headset for questions from any of my staff, a large, dark shape lingers near the entrance to the room.

Eagle.

Always discreet, hovering in the background and keeping an eye on the activities.

I'm just finishing a call from the front desk about a guest who wants to check in but didn't reserve a room, when a well-dressed man lightly clears his throat in front of me.

"Lacey." He says my name in a tone he has no business using at my place of employment, then leans in to kiss my cheek as if we're in France and not Florida. I resist the temptation to roll my eyes. Dylan fucking Acosta. The father of the bride and the shittiest of shitty liars. His smile is deep and warm and totally phony. "You look stunning, as always. Maybe even more so than I remember. And I have very fond *memories*."

I compose my face into an expressionless mask, refusing to give him even a fake smile. "Congratulations, Dylan," I tell him. "I hope you have a wonderful weekend. If you'll excuse me, I'm working." I turn to leave, but he stops me with a hand on my elbow.

The look I give that hand should shred every bit of his cocky confidence. It seems to work, as he has the good sense to remove his hand from my skin, and his face falls for just a moment. What the hell. Did he expect I'd be happy to see him?

"Lacey, I…"

I lost fourteen months of my life to this dirtbag. That is a tiny fraction of the time he has been married to the mother of his children. And still, fourteen freaking months is a long time to live a lie. A very long time to string someone along, only to stomp on their heart. I'm not about to put myself under his heel again.

"Dylan," I say, lowering my voice in warning. "This weekend is about giving your daughter and her fiancé a fantasy. If you say or do anything to piss me off, I will give your family something to remember this weekend by." I smooth the dark purple pocket square that peeks from his jacket pocket, like I'm doing it to be nice. I'm not. I lean in very close and look him dead in the eyes. "Don't give me even the slightest reason to make a scene. It won't be a pleasant one."

I turn away from him and storm toward the kitchen, feeling an intense stare following me.

Once I'm in the kitchen, I huff a massive sigh and curse under my breath. My heart is pounding in my chest, but not because I'm happy to see him. I'm so, so mad at myself for being an idiot.

I square my shoulders and look over the kitchen stations from the doorway like I have a reason to be here other than calming myself down.

The kitchen is a frenzy of activity. Courses being plated, the familiar sounds of steam and sizzling, bubbling pots and chefs calling orders. It's reassuring. Business as usual. Everything here is under control. Unlike my body—and apparently, my heart as well.

I pull in a breath, the scents of garlic and potatoes and roasted beef soothing me. This is good. What we do here is good. I love this job, even if love can't always be trusted and if people are sometimes shit.

I'm an event planner, and I have an event to run. A once-in-a-lifetime beautiful event.

When I head back into the villa, I keep one eye

peeled for Dylan. I need to know where he is at all times so I can stay the fuck away.

I'm so fixated on finding Dylan, I don't see Eagle. But I feel him when a tattooed hand hovers at my elbow, close but not touching me. Suddenly, that bedroom voice is growling against my ear.

"You good?" he asks. "You peeled outta here so fast, you practically burned tire tracks into the floor."

He towers a good three inches above me, and I'm five-eleven in my heels. Without meaning to, without even realizing what I'm doing, I lean against his side. It's a momentary move, the clean, pressed black dress shirt he wears just skimming my bare arm. At our contact, electricity dances along my skin, hitting me like a glass of ice water to the face. I realize what I'm doing and step away from him.

"Sorry. Yeah. I'm good." I scurry away from him, feeling like a billiard ball bouncing across a pool table and banking off not one but two men I'm trying to avoid.

Tonight is so not the night to lust after the biker. No night is the night for that, but tonight, especially. With Dirtbag Dylan in my peripheral vision and Eagle glaring down the guests, I glance at my watch to check the time.

Shit.

Three more hours of this torture to go.

By the time the rehearsal dinner is over, I feel like a deflated volleyball. Dylan's tried two more times to corner me.

First, at the dessert table, where I swear he offered to feed me an egg custard until I threatened to smash it in his face. And since that didn't convince him to behave, he chased me down a second time at the bar when I was trying to order a soda. I was desperate for a hit of sugar and caffeine until I smelled Dylan's expensive cologne way too close for comfort. I whirled away, still thirsty and thoroughly pissed.

If he tries even one more thing, I am gonna make good on my threat to make a scene. We have two more days ahead of us, and I can't helicopter through it. I just hope that when the big event happens, he'll be too busy doing what he should be doing as the father of the bride to harass me.

I can't let one shitty man cost me my job. So, I've done my level best to glare, stare, and beware of him most of the night.

And thank God, this night is officially over.

Once the meals are cleared and the guests are finishing off coffee and dessert, I step outside for a breath of fresh air. My work here is almost done, so I click the button on my walkie-talkie and let the head of hospitality and the kitchen manager know I'm taking a ten-minute break.

It's nearly ten o'clock, and the lights over the koi pond reflect on the smooth surface like floating stars. I lean my elbows against the railing and let my eyes flutter closed. Everything about this night has been exhausting, as I expected it would be.

For the event staff, it's our chance to meet the guests closest to the bride and groom, to understand any unusual requests or limitations the family might have, and to note any changes we might need to make so the wedding itself goes more smoothly. I did all that and managed to ping-pong my way past Dylan, who seemed to be everywhere and constantly too close. I deserve a hot bubble bath and a massage.

I bend a knee and lift one heel out of my shoe to give my toes a rest, when I feel a hand snake along my waist.

"Fuck, you look beautiful tonight. I can hardly keep my eyes off you."

I stiffen and spin to confront Dylan, moving so fast, I step completely out of my shoe. Wobbling on one heel, I put up a hand to push the man an arm's length distance away from me.

"What the hell did I tell you?" I seethe. "Don't you have an ounce of respect?"

My words come out hot and fast—and so loud, I am afraid I shouted them. But at this point, screw this jerk. If Botox Barbie finds out he is a cheater at their daughter's wedding, that is so not my problem.

I stab a finger toward his chest. "Can you try to keep it in your fucking pants while your wife is literally right across the room? Your not-at-all-dead wife, I might add," I hiss.

Dylan's expression goes from suggestive to shocked. "You don't have to be such a bitch," he says, reaching for my hand and pulling me close. "I don't know what your problem is, Lacey. I was simply paying you a compliment. I'm a guest of this establishment, and I would expect you to act with the courtesy the Lantana is known for."

"My issue, Dylan, is you," I say, tugging my hand away from his. Once, his touch felt welcoming, but now, I feel nothing but cold fury. "I told you to stay the hell away from me, but you won't stop. And, yes, you *are* a guest at this establishment. Nothing more, not to me. So, I'd appreciate if you'd act like a guest and not some horny teenager who can't help following me around and making inappropriate little comments."

He doesn't loosen his grip on my wrist. In fact, he tightens it, and I wince at the burn against my skin. "You want to talk about inappropriate, Lacey?"

He's baiting me. I have no idea what he thinks I might have done that's inappropriate, but I have a feeling I'm about to hear it.

"Is this how you dress for all your rehearsal dinners? Fucking tits practically falling out of your dress. Fuck-me heels? You're trying to tell me this little show you're putting on isn't all about me?"

"You're not doing this to me right now," I insist, trying to wrestle my arm away without tipping over on the one high heel I'm still wearing. "This is my place of business. I work here," I bite out. "Your daughter and future-son-in-law are fifty feet away. Your entire family. What I wear and how I conduct myself is my business, not yours." I try to appeal to any shred of decency this man might have. That's a big if, though, as he confirms when he threatens me right to my face.

"It *is* your place of business, and unless you want to find yourself looking for a new job, I'd suggest you stop being such a fucking tease and be a little fucking cordial with your guests. Especially one who's paying the kind of money I am for a prestige experience here."

Prestige experience? I am about to tell him exactly the kind of prestige experience he deserves when someone steps up behind him, and the words die on my lips.

"Mr. Acosta."

The boom of the voice hits Dylan like a kick to the back of the knees. I see him flinch, first looking pissed at the intrusion, but then, as he turns and faces the angry mountain that is Eagle's chest, I can see Dylan's shoulders sag in his expensive suit.

"Is there a problem, friend?" Dylan's voice is tight. He sounds like an entitled prick who's been caught with his hand in the cookie jar, and yet he still thinks it deserves to be there.

Eagle twirls his index finger in the air, motioning to the empty garden. "Listen good, Mr. Acosta. First, you ain't my friend. But you are one of the guests, and from what I can see, you're a pretty important guest, as far as the bride and groom are concerned. Now, I wouldn't normally risk embarrassing one of Lantana's guests, let alone the father of the bride, so I hope like hell I'm mistaken."

He takes a step closer to Dylan, and I can see past

Dylan's shoulders that Eagle's nostrils are flared, his teeth bared like an animal ready to bite.

"I hope I didn't just see you lay hands on Ms. Mercer. I'd be real wrong if I thought there was anything funny going on out here, wouldn't I?" Eagle crosses his thick arms over his chest and cocks his chin. "Tell me I'm wrong, sir, because I'd hate to have to break one of your more important bones the night before you're supposed to walk your baby girl down the aisle."

CHAPTER 4
EAGLE

WELL, I didn't get myself fired for nearly refusing to wear a tux, but threatening the father of the bride at the rehearsal dinner might just be the thing that does it.

I'm waiting for this shit-stain of a man to explain himself or get the fuck out, and lucky for him, he makes the right decision.

"Call off your fucking dog, Lacey," the man seethes, throwing a glare over his shoulder at her.

I resist the urge to snarl at him as he walks by, just to prove his point, but I suppose I should be happy the handsy dickhead is on his way. I wait until he's almost back to the villa before turning to Lacey. I walk the few steps between us, bend, and pick up the shoe she's stepped out of. I set it on the ground near her foot, the sole down against the stamped concrete path, then step away.

I point to the high heel. "Most women want to be swept off their feet, but I don't think that's what that means."

She looks from me to her shoe and then flushes, a light rose blossoming over her throat. I reach out my hand, and she sets her fingers in mine, her touch so light while she balances. She steps into her shoe, rolls her shoulders, and then meets my eyes. "Yeah," she says, sighing. "That's not at all what I want. But, Eagle, thank you."

She looks like she wants to say something when a chirp from the receiver clipped to her dress calls her away.

"I have to go." She nods at me, talks into the receiver, then storms back into the villa.

I follow a few steps behind, scanning the room. A couple of kids from the wedding party ask if they can keep drinking, so I stand beside the bar, a stern look on my face as the bartender explains that tonight, the grounds close strictly at half past ten. My presence keeps the more persistent partiers from trying to get around the policy, so I keep the pissed-off bouncer look plastered on my face while I keep one eye on that jackass father of the bride.

Even while I'm watching him, he's doing everything in his power to prove he's got a death wish. He stares at Lacey's every move, watching her ass when she bends to clasp the hand of an old lady, staring at her face when her mouth lifts in a smile as she says goodnight to the bride. When the asshole's poor wife finally laces a hand through his elbow and tugs him toward the door, I swear he's still looking back over his shoulder, searching the room for Lacey. I weave my fingers together until the knuckles audibly crack, just jonesing for the chance to sink a fist into the nose of that blowhard.

But not now. Not unless he deserves it. That would be the end of my job—and the end of this little thing I've got going with my boss. Whatever this little thing of ours is.

The bartender, a nerdy, skinny dude named Marc, points to a bottle of whiskey. "Thanks for keeping the kids in line tonight. Gonna be a long weekend with this group. You want one for the road, buddy?"

I like Marc. He's good people, and if this were like most nights, I'd grab a drink and shoot the shit with him and Brute for a bit before hitting the road. But Brute's already walking up to say goodbye, and I don't feel like drinking alone.

"Nah, man, but thanks."

Marc nods and busies himself behind the bar, while Brute rolls his neck and yawns.

"You sure you can't stick around a while?" I ask, clapping my hand to my brother's shoulder.

"Nah," he says, giving mine a shake. "Crow's got me on an early job with him. I gotta grab a couple hours of sleep." He releases my hand and looks at me. "I'll put in a word if you want to pick up some laborer shit. Nothing tricky, man. I'm tearing out a kitchen and hauling debris tomorrow. Easy day, good pay."

"Nah." I shake my head. "I'm all right," I tell him. I got no problem with any of my brothers working together, but I'm inching toward fifty. After all night on my feet, I won't be in any mood to get up at the ass-crack of dawn, haul debris out of a kitchen renovation, and then spend tomorrow night on my feet again for the wedding. I'm getting way too old for that kind of schedule, no matter how much I like extra cash. "See ya, man."

Brute takes off, and I turn back to the bar when I hear a soft voice beside me.

"Marc, I'll take a soda, please."

"You want a shot in that, boss?" Marc grins as he packs a glass full of ice and squirts a fizzy nozzle over the ice. Then he runs a lemon wedge along the lip of the glass, squeezes the rind between two fingers so the slightest bit of citrus oil wafts in the air, and slides the wedge over the rim of the glass. "Just the way you like it."

Marc sets the drink down for Lacey, and she reaches a long, bare arm across the bar to grab it. She looks at me, an apologetic smile lifting the corners of her sexy red lips. "I like it with extra ice," she explains. "The lemon bit makes it feel fancy. That's a Marc thing. I'm not really that pretentious."

I never thought she was pretentious, but I don't say anything. I just watch as she drops onto a stool next to me, the sharp edge of her straight blond hair bobbing just past her chin. "You mind if I sit?" she asks. "Long night."

I shake my head slowly, then motion to Marc. "Can I get one of what she's having, but without the frou-frou shit?"

Marc laughs and pours a tall class of soda, extra ice, no lemon, and hands it to me. I nod my thanks and take a long sip, staring ahead into the mirror mounted behind the bar. It feels safer than looking at Lacey, who's crossing her legs and sipping her Coke, sighing like she's releasing the weight of the world from her shoulders.

Our eyes meet in the mirror, and she looks away too fast, like she's embarrassed or feeling guilty.

"I didn't thank you. For earlier," she says quietly, flitting a look at Marc. "Mr. Acosta was getting a little friendly out there. He's a bit of an ass, if I'm honest. But you…" She trails off, then turns a little in her bar seat to face me. "You saved me from having to embarrass him or myself."

I take a long sip, hoping the ice cools down the heat that's radiating between me and Lacey and the renewed rage I feel at the idea that Acosta was, in fact, harassing her.

"Don't mention it," I assure her. "Just doing my job."

She chuckles softly. She motions toward the stool next to her. "Sit?" It's a question, gentle but clearly inviting. "No need to stand while you drink. Besides, I think the grandmas have all made it back to their rooms. You're done for the night."

She doesn't have to ask me twice. I climb onto a stool beside her, my legs spread wide. I rest my left hand on the bar, while I hold my drink in my right one. I drain the glass with just a few sips and set the empty on the bar.

Before I realize what's happening, Lacey trails one short, perfectly polished red nail over the top of my hand, the one that's got as many scars on it as tattoos.

"Would you really have broken his bones?" she asks quietly. "If he'd touched me?"

She lightly touches the tiny, healed marks, pulls her hand away and rests it in her lap as if realizing what she's doing. "Sorry," she whispers. "Speaking of touching, I shouldn't have done that."

She flicks a worried glance up at Marc, but he's got his back to us as he closes up the bar for the night.

I turn a bit on my stool and study her face, the way her lips are slightly parted, the melted chocolate of her eyes. I don't say anything, don't respond to her apology. This is the second time she's touched me, and I know enough about women to know they don't touch men they don't want to touch. Not once—and definitely not a second time.

I wait to say anything until Marc isn't behind the bar anymore. Once he goes off toward the kitchen or doing whatever shit he's got to do so he can close up and call it a night, there's no one around to hear what I want to tell her.

"Lacey." I growl her first name. I normally call her boss—keeping it light, formal. But I like the way her name feels against my lips. I'd like to know how the woman attached to the name feels against my lips too. "You need me for anything, and I mean anything, all you have to do is say the fucking word. And you never have to apologize for touching me."

I don't look away, and neither does she. We're locked in an epic stare-down, the tip of her tongue trailing absently over her lower lip, like she's seriously considering my words.

"The way that fucker looked at you all night, followed you around like a lovesick puppy…" I sniff hard and clench my hands into fists. "I was itching to teach him to keep his eyes to himself. But when he touched you?" I shake my head and pinch my fingers together to show her how close I was to blowing up. "I was *this* close," I tell her, "to adding a couple more black marks to my employment record. Not to mention a couple more scars to these hands."

She swallows hard and sips her drink, her fingers twirling the little lemon wedge around the rim of the glass. "You noticed that, huh?" Her question isn't an accusation. She sounds relieved.

I turn fully on the tiny-ass stool to face my boss. This woman who's probably half my age, but who I've seen hold her own with drunks and dickheads over the last two years. She's as tough as they come when she needs to be, but catch her in the right moment, and she's open, a delicate butterfly with its wings spread to the sky.

Looking at her now, I see how hard she's struggling to pull a mask around herself, to hide in a cocoon of being brave, but the raw emotion in her eyes is clear.

I meet her stare with my own. "I notice everything about you, Lacey."

She presses her red lips together and wriggles in her seat, uncrossing then crossing her legs again. Another flush blooms across her chest, and goddamn, I can't stop myself from looking. I let myself trace the outline of her collarbone to the hollow of my throat with my eyes, then stop myself when my gaze hits her cleavage. I'm overcome by the desire to press my face to her chest, lifting the weight of her breasts in my hands and tasting, feasting on all that hides beneath that black dress.

Lacey must be some kind of a mind reader because I swear I see her flick a look at the erection that's starting to tent the front of my dress pants. She clears her throat. "Eagle, I-I..." she stammers, but no real words come out. Then she slides off the tiny stool, her body so close to me, I smell jasmine and vanilla wafting from her heat.

"Eagle, excuse me," she whispers. "I have to go." Then she takes off in the direction of the ladies' room.

CHAPTER 5
LACEY

AS SOON AS I hit the ladies' room, I yank off my earpiece, unclip the receiver, and drop down on the sofa in the lounge.

"Fuck," I mutter, adjusting in my seat. Five minutes talking to Eagle and all I can think about is having sex with him.

I stand from the sofa and splash cold water on my face, grateful all the guests have left. I run my wet hands over the back of my neck to cool down, when I hear a light knock on the bathroom door.

"What the hell?" I storm through the sitting room, concerned and more than a little confused. I yank the door open, relieved not to see Dylan. And incredibly stunned to see Eagle, his dark dress shirt filling the doorway. "Eagle? What are you..."

He doesn't say anything. Doesn't even blink. He looks from me to the mirrors that line the ladies' room lounge, and before I know what I'm doing, I'm pulling him inside and flipping the dead bolt on the lock.

He's on me in a second, shoving his hands beneath my hair to cup the back of my neck. "Am I wrong?" he asks, his lips against my ear. "Do you want this? Tell me if you don't want me as much as I fucking want you."

My eyes flutter shut, and I practically throw myself against his chest. I swallow back every hesitation, every rational thought about why this is wrong, why we shouldn't do this. Yes, he's my employee. Yes, I know we're at my place of employment. My job. With security cameras that no doubt caught him letting himself into the ladies' room. But the door is locked, and right now, I would much, much rather have him quench the throbbing need between my legs than the silicone I've got waiting at home.

"I've wanted you for so, so long," I say, reaching to lace my hands behind his neck. I scratch my nails through the short hairs on the back of his head, and he groans, lowering his face to mine.

Our first kiss isn't the demure kiss of a bride and groom. It's ravenous and needy, our mouths pressing hard against each other, his lips crushing mine until they feel swollen and raw. I pull back only when I'm desperate for air, panting through parted lips and scraping the tips of my teeth against the scruff on his chin. He tastes so good. His mouth is sweet and almost smoky, like the aroma of coffee without the bitterness.

I grab his face, raking my fingers over the scrub of stubble that gives his dimpled chin texture. My nipples harden, yearning to feel my softness against that firm jaw, those perfect lips. When he cups my ass and presses my hips to his, I release a groan so throaty and deep, I'm almost embarrassed.

But I shouldn't be. Eagle chuckles and meets my groan with one of his own.

"Lacey." That bedroom voice makes my name sound new, sound like the most erotic and beautiful word I've ever heard. "You are so fucking gorgeous..." He pants his praise against my neck, bending his mouth to devour me. He kisses, licks, and nips my throat, the light stubble of his chin scraping my skin and leaving behind the most delicious burn.

I'm writhing with desperation for more, more of him. More of this. I lift his face with my hands, and he slams my body against the wall, bracing a knee between my legs as he explores my mouth with his tongue. We fit together like two halves of one whole finally reunited.

He tastes like heaven—sweet like soda and a little salty—a perfect flavor against my tongue. We kiss and groan, huffing hot breath and banging our backs against the wall as we press every inch of our bodies together. I squirm with need, the ache for him so deep, if he moves his knee just a little higher, I'd grind out a climax against him.

"You're fucking filthy," he pants, pulling his face from mine. "And I love it. I want to watch your face in the mirror while I fuck you from behind."

I open my eyes, my lids so sluggish and heavy with arousal, I have to struggle to peek at him through my lashes. "What?" I mumble, immediately missing his mouth.

"On the couch," he orders, pointing a tattooed finger.

I look at the rose-colored velvet settee and wonder how the hell I'm going to explain ruining it to the facilities staff. Because I have no doubt if I let Eagle get me on that couch, we're going to do unspeakably dirty things to it.

"Hold on," he says, following my eyes. He unbuttons his shirt so fast that I hardly register what he's doing until his sculpted chest is bare, and he's laying the shirt over the seat of the couch. "I'm about to make a big fucking mess eating your pussy."

My knees go so weak at his words that I nearly stumble, but he's got me around the waist and is steering me toward his shirt. When I'm standing in front of the sofa, he kneels and puts his hands on the exposed skin of my thighs. "You want this, Lacey? Because if you don't, say—"

"Fuck me," I beg. "Eat me, fill me. I don't care. I want it all. Give me everything." It occurs to me that I should ask if he has a condom before I tell him he can have his way with me. Before I can form the question, he's pulling his wallet from his back pocket. He opens the trifold and pulls out not one, but three foil packets. A nervous giggle comes over me. "You really keep those in your wallet?"

He tosses the condoms onto the sofa beside his shirt and lifts a brow at me. "I'm old-school, and I've been praying I'd get the chance to do this for the last two years."

I almost gasp at his admission, but before I can say

anything more, his warm hands find their way up my thighs and under my dress. He hooks his fingers into the waistband of my thong. He's so gentle tugging it past my ass that I have to reach under my dress and yank it off for him.

I drop back onto his shirt, a little shy about sitting on the fabric. "Are you sure you don't care about this shirt—"

"Ruin it," he orders, his bedroom voice filling the silence of the lounge. He pushes the fabric of my dress to my waist, still kneeling on the floor. "Sit and open for me, baby. Show me how bad your pussy wants me."

I do as he says, sitting gingerly on his dress shirt and opening my thighs. I haven't had sex with anyone since Dylan, and I haven't exactly trimmed myself much, but if hair bothers Eagle, he doesn't show it. He sucks in a breath, and his bright-blue eyes darken as he flares his nostrils and breathes me in.

"Fuck," he groans. "You're so wet."

"I've been like this all night," I admit.

"You this wet for me?" he asks, taking the tip of one finger and teasing a trail up my thigh and through my curls.

My hips buck at the light contact, and I lift my ass, trying to get closer to him.

"Nuh-uh," he says, withdrawing his fingers. "Answer the question, and I'll take good care of you, baby. You wet for me?"

I snap my eyes open and meet his gaze. "Yes," I breathe. "I want you so damn bad, please…"

"Good answer," he says, returning his fingers to my

pussy. Every light touch of his fingers is a brutal tease. I want him inside me, filling me, but he takes his time, studying my body and fingering his way through my arousal until he finds my clit. I throw my head back against the sofa and spread my legs wider, parting my thighs with my hands.

"Eagle," I say, his name shuddering through my breaths. "For God's sake."

He slides two fingers inside me, then pulls his fingers out and licks them. He curses under his breath, a stream of hot, panting words I can't make out through the haze of lust and heat. "Sweet as fucking honey," he grunts.

He lowers his face between my legs, kneading the muscles of my thighs with his hands and licking long, slow strokes across my clit. I'm panting, moaning, and gripping the crisp dress shirt under my ass between my fingers, lost to the bliss of his mouth on me.

I want to come, but I won't. I need him to fill me, need him deep and hard and fast if he's going to hit that spot to send me to the stars. I tell him I want him inside me, that I need to feel him, and he curses again.

But this time, it's not from arousal.

"Old knees," he laughs, bracing himself on the couch and groaning as he stands up.

I want to help, offer him a hand or anything, but I'm useless. My legs are like syrup, slow and thick and hot as he helps me to stand.

"Tits," he says, that single word sending another tidal wave of heat through me.

With my dress already pushed up to my hips, all I have to do is shove the front of the dress down and my breasts will fall free. I wear this dress so often, I had a strapless bra sewn into the top, so when I push down the material, my breasts rest on top, looking massive and full.

"Jesus Christ," he mutters, his eyes widening. He grabs my hand, then bends to suck a nipple into his mouth. Sparks shoot off behind my eyelids, and I gasp, gripping his massive shoulders and clawing against his smooth back, bringing him closer.

"Turn," he says, pointing at the vanity counter. The entire lounge area is lined with mirrors, so now that I'm standing and my eyes are open, I can see us. Really see us. My dress looks as tiny as a bandanna; the bodice is pushed low, and the skirt is pushed high to cover my belly. Every other inch of my flesh is exposed, revealed to him. In the mirrors that I have looked in so many times that I can see a thousand reflections of myself over the years in my memory.

For a split second, I really think about what we're doing, and it hits me hard.

I'm naked in the ladies' room of the Lantana.

I work here.

This is my dream job.

My nipples are exposed and so erect they hurt, and a massive flush has stained my cleavage a dusky rose color. But this is where I work. This shouldn't be happening. This can't be happening.

My mind starts to race. This is a bad decision. Not just another bad decision in a string of bad decisions.

This is like, what the fuck am I doing, have I lost my mind bad.

It all hits me like a bucket of water.

If I want to stop this, now is the time.

"I want to watch your face when I make you come," Eagle says, nodding toward the counter.

I should have used those useless brain cells when I had the chance, because as soon as he says those words, I'm boneless, thoughtless, too far gone to stop what's happening. Maybe nothing bad will happen. Maybe no one will ever know. There are no security cameras inside the bathroom, and the door is locked. Isn't it?

But then the what-ifs fill my brain...

I'm bent forward, my face so close to the mirror, I leave a hot little circle of mist on the glass when I pant.

I can hear Eagle unzip and then hear the foil wrapper tearing. I feel his hands on either side of my thighs, like he's lining himself up to slide inside me, and fuck, I want this. I don't want to stop. I don't want this pleasure to end. But I love my job, and I know with all my heart that if there is anything that could get me fired—and right now, I'm afraid there are many things that might—letting Eagle take me from behind in the ladies' room would do it.

This is a line I cannot cross.

I've made enough bad decisions. I don't want to make one more. I've lost too many dreams to toss away what little I have for even the mind-blowing orgasm I know I'll have with this man.

Looking in the mirror, I meet his eyes and whisper his name. "Eagle... I don't think..."

He must sense a shift in me as I feel him tense behind me.

His mouth opens, and he tightens his hold on my thighs, but not in a bad way, not like Dylan gripped me earlier. He kneads my muscles, and he lowers his face to whisper against my hair.

"Fuck," he breathes, panting hard against me. I know he put the condom on already, and I feel like shit. We shouldn't stop. But we can't keep going. "Did I hurt you?" he asks. "Fuck it, Lacey, what did I do?"

"No." I give him a wooden smile, no heart behind it. I feel like exactly what Dylan called me. A tease. But I know I'm not doing this to be cruel or to toy with him. So, I tell him the truth. "This job, it's all I have. I mean that. This job means everything to me, and this... We can't."

Eagle closes his eyes for a second, and then he does something that almost breaks me. He draws in a shaky breath, then plants a kiss on the back of my head. After that, he leans back, his hot thighs no longer pressed against mine. He quickly peels the condom from his cock—and oh God, once I get a good look, I'm hating myself for what I'm missing out on—and tucks it neatly back into the foil wrapper.

"Got it. This never happened," he says quietly. Then he tucks the condom into his pants pocket, pulls his shirt from the settee, and shrugs it on.

I am yanking my dress back over my bare ass, and I don't see the look on his face as he dresses. I can't talk to him now, not with my tits out and my pussy still soaked from his mouth. As soon as I'm decent, I'll apologize. I'll…I don't know, offer to make it up to him. I've never been in this situation before. I've never been so reckless and mindless—and I don't think I've ever been so damned turned on. I've made a lot of bad choices, but none that have ever felt this good.

But I don't get the chance to explain or even to tell him I'm sorry. That I would go there with him in a heartbeat if we weren't at my place of employment and if he weren't technically my employee—even though he's a contractor and not actually a Lantana employee.

But I don't get the chance to say any of that. As soon as his shirt is buttoned, without even a look at me, he reaches for the door, unlocks it, and says, "Goodnight, boss," and rushes out of the ladies' room.

CHAPTER 6
EAGLE

IF THIS IS the last weekend I'm employed by Villa Lantana, at least I'm going out in style. For all my resisting and bitching, this overpriced tux does feel like luxury. For a guy who lives in leathers and denim, I gotta admit, this thing feels fantastic. Too bad I can't say the same for me.

Last night, I couldn't even get myself off. After leaving Lacey in the ladies' room, I drove home, replaying the whole fucking thing in my head. I know what she said. She loves her job, blah, blah. But what she didn't say is the same goddamn refrain I've heard over and over in my life.

No, Eagle.

Not you, Eagle.

You're not good enough, Eagle.

She didn't say those words, but she might as well have. My fucking cock was out. My dick was in my hands and about to slide inside her, and she stopped it. She didn't think to stop me on that couch. My shirt still smelled like pussy when I balled it up and threw that shit into the bottom of the hamper.

She didn't stop me when I kissed her, when I sucked her tits. But that's the story of my life. I get this close to something really, really good, and it all gets pulled away.

I get that Lacey is my boss. I'm her employee. And I'm no corporate asshole, but I'm sure there're laws about fucking your boss or some shit. But still, she said no. No to me. And the fact that I almost went there with the woman I've been lusting after for months—scratch that, years now—makes the rejection cut that much deeper.

I should know by now what to expect from women, but I'm a damned fool. After Linda... Fucking Linda... I should have sworn off women for good. At least anything more than fucking them. But apparently, I can't even get that much right.

When I finally arrive for the wedding, I worry for a split second that things might be awkward between Lacey and me. But when I lay eyes on her, I know it's going to be way, way worse than awkward. It's going to be torture.

Brute and I had to wear tuxes, but I put no thought whatsoever into what that meant for Lacey. When I see her, her discreet radio clipped to the dramatic low back of her dress, I know for a fact that the bride's going to feel like shit when she walks down the aisle. Poor woman. Nobody wants to be outdone on their wedding day. And ain't no way anybody's going to be looking at the bride while Lacey's in the room.

When I first see her walking into the chapel, I can tell it's her from the rear. And no, it's not the radio that gives it away. I'd recognize that perfect ass anywhere, and the way it's tightly sheathed in the skin-hugging lavender gown...

Fuck.

I should have asked that seamstress to give me a little extra room in the crotch. Even with humiliation fresh in my mind, my body wants what it wants, and I want Lacey Mercer.

The sun has begun to set as the guests gather for the ceremony. Brute is standing by the pond, yawning into his fist and tugging on the collar of his expensive-ass shirt. I nod at him as I join him.

"How was the gig?" I ask.

"Easy," he says. "But that don't mean I ain't ready for a couple hundred hours of sleep."

I nod. "Been thinking about what you said."

"Yeah? What's that?" Brute asks.

"You think Crow's got room in his crew?"

Brute gives me wide eyes and nods. "Yeah, fuck yeah. You hate the suit that much? You thinking of cutting loose from this cush gig?"

"Maybe," I say with a shrug.

A golf cart is just pulling up to the white stucco chapel. I recognize the groom's grandma and know that means I'm on duty.

"I'll talk to Crow," Brute says. "You serious? He could probably get you on the crew this week. He wanted me Monday, but I told him I needed a day off after working the brunch tomorrow."

"I'll talk to him," I say.

The golf cart comes to a stop, and I leave Brute to offer my arm to Grandma Warner.

"You look beautiful today, ma'am," I tell her. "Congratulations."

The groom's grandma can't be a day under eighty, but she twists her neon-pink lips together and clings to my arm. "Wanna make it a double wedding?" she asks. "I'm not taken…"

"Gram." One of the bridesmaids swoops in and practically peels Mrs. Warner off me. "Let's leave the flirting for after the ceremony, shall we?"

She ushers the old lady into the chapel, but Grandma Warner looks back over her stooped shoulder and gives me a wink so big it's hard not to smile.

Well, at least not all my prospects have dried up.

Just as I'm mentally tearing myself down again, Lacey comes hustling down the path toward the chapel. She's got a tablet in her hands and looks focused on a couple of old ladies who are asking if they can get champagne delivered to the chapel.

She says something to them very quietly but very firmly and sends them off into the chapel in search of seats. I try to pull myself away, spare myself the embarrassment of looking her in the face, but I can't walk away. Not from her. I watch, my feet stuck to the ground like I've been poured into the stamped concrete path. All I can do is cross my arms over my chest and hope I don't rip this expensive-ass suit.

"Hi, Eagle," she says, meeting my eyes. Her lips are vibrant red, and her makeup is sultry, her brown eyes glittering under lids coated with some sparkly looking eyeshadow. Harp music starts up inside the chapel, and I nod at Lacey then start to move out of the way to allow the last of the arriving guests a clear path inside.

"Eagle, may I speak to you, please?" Lacey asks, her voice all business.

My gut tightens as I imagine she's going to tell me off. She'll say last night was an accident. That it can never happen again. That she's my boss, and all the other shit I've been telling myself since I got home last night. I don't want to hear it. I half consider saying no to her, calling Brute over and letting him work the chapel while I look down into the koi pond like he is, not a care in the fucking world.

But I can't. I don't. My brain wants to leave, but my body ain't having none of it.

"Evening." I firm my lips and try to stare past her, but fuck, it's hard. I've never been a romantic. Been married, but never had one of these fancy parties. Linda and I were just teenagers—me with a bad attitude and a worse haircut, and her with what we thought at the time was a late period. The courthouse, some quick signatures, and bam. Before I knew what I signed on for, the bitch I'd been fucking in the back seat of my daddy's work truck was my wife.

That was a lifetime ago, and yet somehow, all the shit I've felt over the years on the roller coaster with Linda comes rushing back at me.

"Eagle." Lacey meets my eyes and lifts her chin. "That tuxedo..." She smooths down one shoulder of the jacket, although I'm not sure it needs it. Then she nods.

"You look as handsome as ever. Gorgeous, in fact. Tom Ford should be proud to dress you."

Well, that's unexpected. I don't smile but study her face as I return the compliment. "You do too," I say cautiously. "As beautiful as always."

She holds up one finger to me and taps the button on her radio. "Mmm-hmm," she says to whoever has called her. "I'll be right in." Then she turns her attention back to me. "Eagle, can I ask you a question?"

"Yeah," I say, braced for anything and having no fucking idea what she's thinking.

She's so tall in her heels, when she leans close, her face almost reaches my ear. "Can we talk later? After the wedding, I mean." She leans back, her smile gone. She looks determined, not at all the flustered woman I've been lusting after for far too long.

"I need to go," she says, nodding toward the chapel. "Let me know later how you feel. I understand if your answer is no." She starts to head into the chapel, but then stops, turns to me, and smiles. "But I hope you'll give me a chance to explain."

I don't say anything. There really isn't anything to say. I don't need an apology, and I sure as hell don't want an explanation. She did what she needed to do, and the last thing I need is to hear some sorry-ass excuse, when what she really means is, yeah, this thing can't happen. I get it. I don't need it shoved in my face by yet another woman.

I look away from her retreating ass and instead look over the guests shifting in their seats. This damn place must cost a fortune. To pay for a wedding here... Fuck.

If they'd spend six grand a piece on tuxes for the damned security guards, then I cannot imagine what a rehearsal dinner, wedding, and day-after brunch cost the Acostas. Mr. Acosta may be an entitled dick, but he's exactly the kind of rich dickhead that someone like Lacey deserves. Probably wants. Even if she might be tempted to scratch an itch with an asshole like me. But apparently not that tempted.

I scan the chapel and then step outside into the fading evening heat. These tuxes are luxurious, but if I'm grateful for anything, it's that the wedding starts late in the day. No bride wants to sweat her tits off on her wedding day, and I sure as shit don't need this tux to become a wet suit.

I tug at the collar and adjust my sleeves, then wander back over toward Brute. That gig working with Crow is sounding better and better.

From my vantage point, the wedding was easy money. The ceremony itself happened at dusk, and since I didn't have to wrangle any drunk groomsmen or jealous bridesmaids, I could keep an eye on things and enjoy the gorgeous sunset. Brute spent a good part of the ceremony on the phone, so I stayed near the chapel, roaming the exterior and discreetly looking in to make sure everything was okay.

For his part, the shit-stain father of the bride didn't do anything to piss me off—which isn't saying much. His wannabe model wife clutched his arm and leaned on him so much, the poor asshole couldn't even swivel his head to stare at Lacey.

But I could.

She stayed discreetly at the back of the chapel, tiptoeing on her heels, tapping at the earpiece, and checking the iPad periodically. She caught me staring at least a half dozen times, but each time, I looked away.

Something about Lacey opens up a part of me that I don't like. The fact that she cut shit short last night between us has gotten under my skin more than I'd like to admit. And I don't like the feeling. I'm the type of guy who bangs hard and leaves early. I don't do relationships—not anymore.

And that works out fine. Most of the women who still hang around at the compound are partnered up to the members now. I miss the days when the pussy was easy and there were no such things as boundaries. But times have changed, and I've had to change with 'em.

Nowadays, I work events here and bounce at a couple local clubs during the week. The pay is easy, and the clubs bring in the college kids, so there is no such thing as a slow night. I know a couple of bartenders who are happy to take me home at the end of the night, and that's been enough.

But somehow, a couple of fumbled kisses and a taste of Lacey's pussy got me thinking harder than I've thought in years. I'm in my mid-forties. The club's gone clean, which means no wild parties anymore, no cash flowing in and out. No guns, no danger, no crime.

And that means the most excitement I get is dolling

up in an overpriced suit and helping Granny safely out of the golf cart.

This is so not the life I expected for myself.

I didn't have a lot of dreams for myself growing up. Nobody I knew did. Truth is, I never expected to live to see thirty, let alone forty. Making it as long as I have? I've way outlived any plans I might have made for myself.

I got married too young, but that was a lifetime ago. I was a different person. Linda and I weren't gonna do things the traditional way.

I was never a guy who had goals or made plans. I never felt worthy of either. And life didn't do me any kind of favors, so why would I change my attitude?

"Yo." Brute's hand on my shoulder stops me from thinking. "What time's this shindig over? You think there's any chance I could knock off a little early?"

He yawns, and I notice how red his eyes are. I glare at him, hoping he's clean and sober. No matter how tired he is, we're on the job. But Brute's like me. He marches to his own beat, so I wouldn't put it past him to have snorted something to keep himself awake after working all day.

I shake my head. "You know the drill by now. Dance floor closes at eleven, and we got to have everybody out by midnight. Why, you gonna turn into a fucking pumpkin?"

Brute snorts a laugh. "Just tired as fuck, bro. I thought I could hack a day on the job and then standing around, but I need a decent meal and some coffee or shit."

I nod. "Go to the bar. Marc'll hook you up. We'll get through it. But you might wanna see if one of the other guys can cover for you tomorrow. We got a lot more weekend ahead."

He nods. "I might just, but I don't know who the fuck'll do it on short notice." He yawns again. "Fuck me. I'll ask around."

That's another problem with having a club that's too settled. Morris always used to be down for anything. Ride or die on a moment's notice. But our VP has kids now and runs a business of his own. Weekends are family time. I chuckle just thinking that. Who'd ever have thought the club would have legit businesses.

"Try Leo or maybe Arrow," I say.

Leo's the newest patch, but he's got a small kid, so he's probably not down for a Sunday gig. But Arrow and his girlfriend Annie don't have anything tying them down.

"Arrow... I never think about that guy. I'll try him. You got his number?"

Arrow is a former PI who did security for a while. He was working on a case for a woman who was being stalked and threatened. And when the asshole made Arrow as her bodyguard, Arrow and Annie stayed at the compound in Crow's old room while things were hot.

Arrow's no Disciple, but he's good people, and he could definitely handle security at a place like this.

"Check with the boss," I remind him, knowing there's paperwork and shit if he decides to bring someone in to cover for him.

Brute gives me a thumbs-up and heads toward the villa, where they are setting up for a hell of a cocktail party.

I stand back and listen to the final cheers of the guests, as the new Mr. and Mrs. Warner exit the chapel to applause. Since it's already dark out, instead of throwing birdseed at the happy couple, they all carry little battery-powered tea lights and walk as a big group toward the villa for the cocktail hour.

It's hard not to be moved by it, all those people carrying all those small golden lights through the twilight. I wonder if that was one of Lacey's ideas. Even the grandmas get in on it, leading the guests in the golf cart, waving their tea light candles in the air like they are at a rave. My cold, dead heart warms a little at that, especially since Grandma wags a finger at me in a come-hither gesture as she passes by.

After the last of the guests has left the chapel, Lacey comes out, thanks the officiant and the minister and then calls for the grounds keeper to lock up the chapel. She flicks a look at me as she scurries toward the villa, but I look away, distracted by a small commotion coming from just outside the villa.

Lacey seems to notice it at the same time I do. We swap a quick look, just seconds before I hear a loud shout.

"Fuck you, Dylan."

And then I hear the unmistakable sound of someone being slapped, and I take off running.

CHAPTER 7
LACEY

ALL I KNOW IS that Dylan must have had it coming. That's what I first think when I hear someone shout at Dylan and then slap him.

Eagle is running toward the scene before I can even react. But I can tell immediately from the dress that the woman beside him is wearing that the person who delivered the slap that rang out across the property is none other than the mother of the bride.

I hurry over to see what the hell is happening. "Olivia?" I call. "Is everything all right?"

Dylan has a hand to his mouth, and I cannot believe it, but his lip is actually bleeding. My stomach sinks. Olivia Acosta is wearing a couple of huge rings on her fingers. I don't know how she did it, but she actually hurt her husband.

By the time I get there, Eagle is speaking to Olivia in a low, calming voice.

"Ma'am, why don't you come inside, and I'll get

you some water." He's trying to step between Olivia and Dylan, but Dylan is seething, sputtering, and not doing anything to try to calm the situation.

My arrival only makes things worse. So much worse.

"Fuck you too. Fuck you, Lacey. How dare you." Olivia is gesturing at me, and I swear if Eagle weren't between them, she looks as if she'd slap me too.

"Mrs. Acosta," I say, starting to freak out. What the hell happened? What am I missing, and why do I feel like I'm about to be sick?

The guests have all filed inside to get their drinks, but soon, people will fill the gardens to mingle for the cocktail hour. Plated appetizers will be served, and nothing that goes on here can be kept quiet. We only have a few moments before there's a scene that really will make this a night to remember.

"Do you need someplace private to talk? I can offer you and Mr. Acosta my office," I say, desperate to do something, anything that will ease this situation down from what feels like the brink of a code-red emergency.

Dylan is blotting at the blood on his lip with the back of his hand.

Eagle suddenly seems to notice the blood. Dylan is hurt. "Does that need to be looked at?" Eagle asks. "We should get some ice on that."

"You can keep the fuck out of things that don't concern you," Dylan says, and before I can defend Eagle, Olivia points a furious finger at me.

"You want to get my husband in your office? Why,

did you fuck him there too? Do you plan to totally humiliate me on my daughter's wedding day? Was that your plan all along?"

As soon as she says the words, a wave of nausea surges from my belly to my throat.

She knows.

She knows.

I don't know how she found out or how this happened now, of all times and of all freaking places... but she *knows*.

Eagle's face goes as red as a tomato, but I look to him desperately for help because I don't know how I'm going to handle this.

It's like everything in my life passes before my eyes. I have a bride and groom about to celebrate the biggest night of their lives, and something in my past, my stupid choices, isn't just going to stress me out. My shitty mistake is about to blow up in my face.

I put a hand to my chest, not sure what to say. How to address the very obvious problem we have, when thankfully, Eagle steps in

"All right," he says loudly enough that Olivia and Dylan both jerk to attention. "I'm only going to say this once," he says, his voice murderously low but crystal clear. "I need everyone here to calm way the fuck down. Do you understand me? No swearing, no hitting, and no accusations. Now, follow me. I'm not going to ask nicely if I have to say it a second time."

I swallow hard against the sour taste in my mouth and watch wordlessly as Eagle lifts a hand and motions to Brute. "I'm taking Lacey and the Acostas for a quick chat. Watch the place," he says.

Brute lifts a dark brow and does a double take at Dylan's bleeding lip, but he nods. "Got it. You need… anything?" he asks, no doubt wondering if Eagle can handle whatever's going down on his own.

"I'm good," Eagle says. Then he turns to me and points. "Your office."

I hear the words, but I'm not sure what he means. I think my brain is frozen or I'm going into some kind of shock. It's like I see every lie Dylan told me playing out in my memory right here like a movie.

His wife fucking knows. And I don't think I have ever felt so ashamed. It was horrifying to find out that none of what Dylan told me was true. But after I broke it off with him, what settled in deep was this sense of shame. Disgust at myself. I let myself be lied to.

I saw those red flags waving, and yet, like a bull, I charged forward, oblivious to the danger I was in.

All of it hits me so fast, I can't move. In my earpiece, I hear the head of catering tell me the appetizers are on their way out, and my knees almost buckle. That means the guests will be coming outside any minute. Whatever composure I have completely leaves my body. My hands go clammy, and suddenly, I drop my tablet. It hits the concrete path and shatters. My hands start to shake, and I gasp, staring between the now-useless device and Olivia, whose overly tanned face is screwed up in a cruel grin.

"Karma's a bitch, isn't it," she hisses, and it's then that my eyes start to burn.

"*Ma'am.*" Eagle's tone sets even my teeth on edge. He is not playing, and even I jump a little at how angry he sounds.

Olivia swivels her gaze to him.

"I told you I wasn't gonna ask twice." Eagle withers her with his glare, and she has the good sense to keep her mouth shut.

He looks at me, and I just blink, staring without really seeing anything. He comes up to me, bends, and picks up the tablet. Then he changes his tone altogether. "Lacey," he says, his voice warm and gentle. "I need you to take me to your office now. Can you do that?"

I nod once.

Yeah, I can do that. I can do this. Maybe not without Eagle, I realize. All my professionalism has just disappeared like dew in the morning sun. I know I am better than this. I know I am stronger, smarter, but in that moment, the shock and the shame take over. I need a moment to collect myself. But I can't walk away from this. I can't escape what I've done.

"Lacey." Eagle's voice is calm but insistent, and I nod, knowing that I have to do this.

I lift my chin and start walking slowly toward the villa. I pick up speed and move faster, and as if there are wheels under my heels, I speed walk past the bar, which thankfully is full of guests laughing and talking, ordering drinks, and way too chatty to notice anything is amiss. At least, I hope they don't.

Normally, I would be listening to their conversations at a polite distance, thrilled to blend into the background and absorb the happiness. I live for those moments. When the friends of the bride say this is the most beautiful wedding they have even been to. When hopeful young couples wonder if they can manage to have their wedding here. When older, long-married couples, infected by the joy and hope that a wedding seems to give everyone, hold hands for maybe the first time in a long time and look at each other, remembering why they are together. How far they have come since they walked down an aisle someplace and made their vows so many years ago.

Those are the moments that give me life, energy, and hope. But today, I truly just want to disappear. No one wants to think about the worst times in a relationship, the worst times in a marriage, at a wedding. It's literally the last thing anyone wants to bring to the party, and I've done that for Olivia just by being here.

This might officially be the worst night of my life.

I clasp my clammy hands and race toward my office. I can hear the heavy footfalls and the low rumble of Eagle talking to Dylan and Olivia, so this bad, bad night is about to get a lot worse.

My office is unlocked, so I shove the door open and head directly to my desk. I plop down in my chair before I fall over and wring my hands in my lap.

I have no idea what happened, what Olivia knows, what Dylan said or did. All I know is the woman whose husband I was sleeping with for fourteen months knows something. And she is inches away from me right now.

My cheeks burn, and the first thing I think is that I need to apologize to her. None of this is my fault, but I did something wrong. I am wrong. I was selfish and needy and let all my better judgment fall by the wayside, and someone got hurt. That's reason enough to do it.

As Eagle is closing the door, I stand up and blurt it out.

"I am so, so sorry," I say, looking at Olivia. But as it comes out, I realize that was the absolute wrong thing to say.

"Fuck you and your apology, you stupid slut." Olivia is pointing at me. "How dare you? How bloody dare you?"

Her use of the word bloody shakes me, and for a moment, I realize it must be some word she's picked up to sound cultured or cool. I know from Dylan that his wife is from Missouri, and I sure as hell don't think they say bloody there. My mouth falls open as I try to think of what to say to settle this situation, but I don't have to.

Eagle starts barking out orders.

"Everybody sit down and shut up. That includes you, Lacey." Eagle points at Olivia and Dylan, but my guests are not about to be intimidated by a biker at their daughter's wedding.

"Excuse me," Olivia says, but there is nothing polite about her tone. "But what gives you the right to get involved here? Do you know this whore slept with my husband? And not just once, although God knows she should have had more than enough of him after one time. They had an affair, and she has the gall, the nerve—"

My cheeks burn, and I feel bile burn the back of my

throat. "It wasn't like that." I try to interrupt, but I didn't eat much today and haven't had anything to drink since lunch. I'm starting to feel light-headed, and I drop into my chair, just hoping against hope that I don't pass out. Although I don't know if even that would make this night any worse.

The moment I hit my chair, Eagle was at my side. "Lacey, you need water. Are you feeling light-headed?"

He takes my hand in his, and I nod, pointing to the small fridge over by the coffee bar. "Water," I whisper.

He charges over to the mini fridge and grabs three waters, then points at Olivia and Dylan.

"I don't know what happened, but what I do know is that we need to get first aid for that." He points to Dylan. "And we need to cool things down just a bit before anything else breaks or anyone else gets hurt."

"Hurting people is his specialty," Olivia sneers, turning away from her husband.

Eagle uncaps the water for me and bends down, keeping his head level with mine while I take a shaky sip. "Good," he encourages. "Just cool off for a few minutes. Deep breaths."

Then he walks over to Dylan and Olivia. I can hear them all arguing, and I catch glimpses of it, but I'm swimming in shame. All I can imagine is how she found out. What she knows. I think of all the text messages I sent Dylan when I thought he was a widower.

Shame sets my face on fire as I think of the pictures and the videos. Oh my God, the videos. What was I thinking?

"Oh God," I moan, and I lift my head long enough to take another sip of water.

I know in some small part of my brain that I should be angry. That I should defend myself, stand up to this woman who, yes, was wronged, but my God. She was wronged not by me, but by her own damn husband. Part of me knows this, but I can't.

Maybe I should have tried to cancel their wedding once I found out Dylan was the father of the bride. Maybe I should have been nicer to him last night... I mean, what if something I said to him set off the chain of events that led to Olivia finding out?

I don't have much time to think this through, because before long, Eagle is standing beside me, holding his hand out to me.

"Lacey," he says gently. "I need you to use that headset of yours and see if you can get somebody to bring us some ice for that busted lip. Can you do that?"

I lift my head and look into his beautiful eyes, the wrinkles around them reminding me of how gorgeous he looked when he was kissing me just last night. My God, my life is a mess.

"Lacey?" Eagle takes my hand in his and squeezes. "I need you to help me here, Lacey. Can you put out a call for some ice?"

The warmth and firm pressure of his hand over mine snaps my body to attention. "Okay. Ice." I nod, every inch of me numb except the fingers laced with his. "Do we need first aid?"

Eagle shakes his head. "Nah, it's a lip, so it bleeds a lot. He'll be fine. We just need to stop the swelling."

I tap the receiver and call out to the bar, asking one of the servers to bring some ice and cloth napkins to my office.

"Tell them to bring some fucking whiskey," Dylan rasps, looking irritated and completely serious.

Olivia huffs, and Eagle gets up, stands over the two of them, and shakes his head. "Neither one of you is getting drunk tonight. Is that clear? And neither one of you is going to ruin this night for your daughter." He holds his hands palms up. "I mean, if the two of you wanna blow this night up and make a scene that will most certainly ruin what I'm sure is a very, very expensive party, be my guest. But if I see one more sign that you're out of control—that means violence, getting trashed, anything—I call the cops. That simple. Disorderly conduct, assault, whatever you want, you do. But I'm not fucking around here. You start anything, and I finish it with a call to 9-1-1. You hear me?"

Olivia sobers for a second, looking down at her ring, the one that I assume cut Dylan's lip. "I can't get arrested at my daughter's wedding. Do you see what you've done?" She then bursts into tears—fake ones, thank God. I think if she seemed really sad, I would have started crying too. But her eyes are dry, and she's making this moaning sound that almost makes me laugh.

Dylan sighs and rubs his head, while Eagle goes to answer the knock at my office door.

He comes back with a large glass filled with ice and two pristine white napkins. "Take this," he says, thrusting everything at Dylan. "Clean yourself up and pull it together."

Dylan looks down at his hands and the blood that's drying on his fingers, then looks helplessly at Olivia. "Would you?" he asks.

And to my utter shock, she stops the crocodile tears, rushes over to him, and starts cooing over his cut.

"We'll tell the kids the back of my ring hit your lip by accident," she says, not even sounding apologetic. She expertly wraps the napkin around the ice and dabs Dylan's lip. "It'll be a funny story."

"They might not even notice," Dylan says, sounding completely chill about the fact that his wife assaulted him on their daughter's wedding day. "It's fine. I'm fine."

"Of course you are," Olivia says, nodding. "We're going to have to ask the Lantana to replace the wedding planner, though. You know that, right?"

"Of course, baby." Dylan flicks a look at me, and in that instant, every bit of guilt I was feeling rises to the surface and is washed away by a wave of anger.

"Wait just a minute," I say, standing from my desk.

Now Eagle rushes toward me, keeping me from getting close to the Acostas, who now seem not like fighters but members of the same team united against a common enemy.

"I did nothing wrong here," I say. "There is no other wedding planner. There is just me."

Olivia sets the bloody napkin down on the edge of my desk, puts her hands on her hips, and lifts a brow at me. "You have an assistant," she says. "And I'm sure with what we're paying for this wedding and the rehearsal and the brunch, the owners will understand if we're not exactly happy with the service you've provided."

"What do you mean?" I ask. "I didn't do anything wrong. Everything has been flawless, perfect..." I trail off. I mean, of course they don't want me around, but...

"Call your supervisor," Olivia says, turning her glare on me. "Now. I'd like you replaced before my daughter cuts her cake. Or I will have my lawyers sue you, this place, and everyone who works here for anything their creative legal minds can come up with."

My mouth drops open, and I try to argue, but Dylan smirks at me. "Don't worry. I've got Sergio Lantana's number. I'll call myself."

I shake my head slowly and take two steps back. Sergio Lantana is the owner, and I have no doubt that Dylan does have his number. That would end me for sure. I'm in over my head, and even though I'm angry, I know I'm out of options here.

"That won't be necessary," I say, my voice cracking over the words. I'm trying not to cry, but I hope I don't sound like it. "I'll call the manager and my assistant. I'll take care of it."

I turn and walk back to my desk, feeling like I've been shot through the stomach. I have no idea what I'm going to say. What I'm going to tell Don, the night manager, about this. How I'm going to explain to Carla, my assistant, that she has to leave her kids on a Saturday night to cover an event because I fucked the father of the bride, and his wife found out.

I don't know how my heart takes the pain shooting through it, but somehow, as Eagle sends Olivia and Dylan back to the party, I know I have no choice. I take off my headset and pick up my desk phone.

"Don?" I say, my voice shaking. "It's Lacey. We have a problem."

CHAPTER 8
EAGLE

I SPENT the rest of the wedding glaring at the bride's parents. Those two give entitlement a run for its money.

The mom had the audacity to make a toast to her husband and joked that she hoped the worst pain her daughter would suffer in her own marriage was the pain of accidentally splitting open her husband's lip. I seethed and it took everything in me not to roll my eyes, but I watched with a tight jaw and even tighter fists as that blowhard piece of crap Dylan gave some speech about the sanctity of marriage and what it takes to make a life with someone.

Lying sacks of shit.

My own wife was no fucking saint. My own marriage ruined me.

What I couldn't burn from my eyes was the look of absolute defeat on Lacey's face. After she called the night manager, Don, he placed a call to Lacey's assistant, and everyone agreed that for the sake of the Lantana's reputation, the best course of action would be for Lacey to take the weekend off and let Carla run the events in her place.

Lacey's face looked as shattered as her tablet screen as she walked slowly from the property to her car, her purse in one hand, her lavender dress clinging to her legs with every slow step.

Brute was so stunned that Lacey had been sent home that I explained the whole shitty story to him. He asked what I was going do about it, as if I had some obligation here. That was when I realized I felt like I did.

I convinced Brute to keep his shift tomorrow, and I fired off a text to Arrow to see if he'd be able to cover the day-after brunch for me. It was a big ask on short notice, but the club has done a lot for Arrow. Even though he isn't a member, if he had two brain cells in that head of his, he'd realize the brotherhood extended him a lot of courtesy at a time when he really needed it. And while I didn't want to say he owed me, it'd say a lot about him if he didn't come through the first and only time I asked for a favor.

I don't like owing people anything, and I sure didn't like calling in a favor that he didn't exactly owe me personally, but the club is all I have. My family, my friends, my brothers. I had to believe one of them would bail me out here, back me up. I mentally ran through the list of who else I could text on short notice just in case Arrow didn't come through.

But Arrow didn't disappoint.

Done, he texted. *You tell me when and where I gotta be and how to dress, man. I'll be there, no problem.*

The reception went off without a hitch. A couple of broken beer bottles on the dance floor were about the most exciting things that happened. And I do think the best man may have puked in the pond, but Brute was out there when it happened, so that was his mess to deal with.

The rest of the night went off without any more scenes or slaps, puking incidents or bleeding—a hell of a lot better than the night started out.

And I'm grateful for that because my mind was working triple time the whole evening. I hardly heard the seven-piece band play a single song, I was too worried about what these fuckers had done or could still do to Lacey.

I was suddenly relieved we hadn't fucked in the ladies' room. I mean, it would have been great, but after seeing how these people act, I have no doubt if someone found us, it would have been even worse for her.

By the time the bride and groom left the dance floor, I had a plan in place. Grandma Warner cozied up to me just as the ballroom lights went back on.

"I know you're working tonight, but I would have loved a dance with you." She waggled her brows at me suggestively. "I may be slower, but I've still got moves."

"I saw you out there, ma'am. I think it's a good thing I was working. I don't think I could have kept up with your moves." I gave her a genuine smile and helped her into the golf cart for the final time.

I kept an eye on the bridesmaids and groomsmen, all the sloppy friends who'd had way too much to drink, knowing they had to stumble just a few hundred yards to their rooms at the resort.

Before the last of the guests even left, Dylan and Olivia Acosta left the ballroom together, arm in arm, heads held high, neither one of them even looking in my direction. That was just fine by me. I hoped I'd never have to see that smarmy asshole or his bitch wife again as long as I lived.

As the clock turns over to midnight, I let Carla know that Arrow is going to cover for me tomorrow, and I won't be in. The poor woman is so frazzled by all the activity, she doesn't even ask questions. She just nods and thanks me for everything I've done.

"Have you talked to her?" Carla asks. "Is Lacey okay?"

I shake my head. "No idea."

I don't say more, don't want to give away any information that anyone might use against Lacey.

Then I look back through my contacts and use the number that Lacey contacted me from to confirm my tuxedo fitting the other day.

It's me, I text. *Eagle. You okay?*

She sends back a crying face emoji, and I have to laugh. I forget how much younger than me she is. I don't have whole conversations by emoji, but sometimes it just works.

Me: You want a shoulder to cry on?

I send the text before I can think better of it, talk myself out of what might be a really, really bad decision.

There is a long wait before I get another text from her. But then she sends it…an address.

I type it into the map app in my phone and then text her back.

Me: I'll be in there in 20 minutes. Tom Ford and all.

I get back a cry-laughing emoji, which I think is an upgrade from just plain crying. Then I fire up my car and search for any late-night pizza joints. I'm famished, and I sure as shit could use a couple of beers after the night we had. I try not to think about the condoms that are burning a hole in my wallet. I'm not going there for that.

But I'd be a liar if I didn't admit that even if Lacey doesn't want me that way, I'd go to her. Just to see if she's okay, I tell myself. Just to see if she needs me to crack open the other side of Dylan Acosta's stupid, rich mouth.

Whatever happens, I want to be there.

I pull up to a small one-story ranch-style house on a quiet street in a very modest neighborhood. I don't see any lights on, and it occurs to me that maybe Lacey doesn't live alone. Dogs, roommate, I don't know. I park on the street and pull out my phone.

Me: I'm out front with pizza and beer.

Faster than I can even believe, a light goes on over a small front door. I take the walkway from the sidewalk that leads up to the cracked front steps and meet Lacey on a weather-worn covered porch. She's locking the front door and motioning for me to follow her around to the back of the house.

"I live with my mom," she explains, taking the beer

from me. "Mom's room is off the front, so if we go in the back, we won't wake her up."

I follow her quietly and wait for her while she unlocks a storm door and a heavy wooden door that leads into a nicely furnished but very small sunroom. Lacey steps aside and lets me pass, then locks the door behind her. She has a sweet setup out here. A small dining table and two chairs are up against the wall closest to the door, and a comfy-looking outdoor sectional sofa with sun-faded cushions faces a very small wall-mounted television. A ceiling fan swirls overhead, moving the cool night air through the screened-in space. It's not huge, but it's a big enough space for a woman and her mother to enjoy.

Lacey sets the beer on the table, and I follow suit, setting down the hot pizza box.

I turn to face her, and before I can get a word out, she launches herself at me. She wraps her arms around me and presses her face against my chest. Without the sky-high heels, she's a lot shorter than me, and I swallow hard, letting her hold me before finally giving in and wrapping my arms around her back. I hold her tight, lowering my head to rest my chin lightly against the top of her messy blond hair.

We're absolutely quiet, nothing but the whir of the fan that sounds as if it's working damn hard to keep the heavy air moving. I breathe in deep, her coconut smell filling my chest. I close my eyes, and neither one of us says anything for a really long time. It should be awkward, but God, it isn't.

When she finally steps back, I can see that she's

wearing a thin T-shirt without a bra. Her nipples are rock hard and pressing against the fabric like they are desperate for release. I can relate to that feeling. My boss's feet are bare, and she's wearing sleep shorts that look at least ten years old.

It's adorable and humbling. She looks wrecked and young—nothing like the capable, confident, sexy-as-shit woman I see at work.

I loosen my tie, suddenly feeling every inch of this suit. "I feel a little overdressed," I admit.

She laughs and wipes at tears that have gathered in the corners of her eyes. "You..." She shakes her head. "Eagle, you look gorgeous. Exactly like I imagined you would."

My breath catches in my chest at her words. She complimented me earlier at the wedding, but I just took that as friendly, encouraging boss-employee talk. I didn't want to wear the tux, and I thought she was being supportive about my giving in and doing it.

But there's no mistaking the sincerity in her voice. She looks so sad, but her lips are curved into a shy smile. And she rakes her eyes over me from head to toe. I stand a little straighter under her gaze, my dick making it very hard for me to ignore how sheer her sleep shirt is.

I clear my throat and realize I have no idea why I'm here. I don't know what I expect. Lacey and I have never hung out. Other than what I felt and tasted fucking around in the restroom last night, I have no intimate or personal knowledge of this woman. I didn't know she lived with her mother. Although, as I scan the place, I see huge dog toys scattered around the floor and a dog bed in one corner that looks big enough for me to lie down on.

"Dog?" I ask, nodding toward the bed.

She sniffles and nods. "German shepherd. She's a huge, lovable furball, but she's very protective of my mom and me."

I nod, liking the sound of that. I haven't even met her mom, but seeing this house and this neighborhood, I find it hard not to feel protective of these women. It's not a bad neighborhood by any means, but it's clearly working-class, nicer than the area I grew up in, but still. Two women alone brings out the instinct in me, and I'm glad they have a dog around.

"Inside with your ma?" I ask.

She shakes her head. "I boarded her with a really great day care place for the weekend. My mom works almost every weekend on the early shift. When I have a three-day event—" she lowers her eyes "—like this one, Ruby would be alone too long otherwise."

"Ruby?" I ask, curious about the name. "Why Ruby?"

Lacey blushes and purses her lips. "It's my favorite stone. I always thought growing up that the prettiest engagement rings were rubies. I never understood why people liked diamonds when you could have a gorgeous red ruby. So, Ruby."

"Makes sense," I say. It occurs to me that she really wasn't kidding about the Lantana being her dream job. If she had strong opinions about engagement rings as a kid, she's probably been wedding-obsessed for a long time. "Better name than my dog had," I say.

I hate telling people about my childhood, but the mood is already low enough, and maybe, just maybe, the story about my dad's dog will give her a laugh.

"You have a dog?" she asks, brightening.

I shake my head. "Nah. I live in the compound, and it's not a pet-friendly kind of place." Although, it could be, seeing as half the time we've got kids and toys where we once had pool tables, half-naked women, and full kegs.

I shrug off my jacket, and Lacey takes it and hangs it carefully over the back of one of the chairs by the table.

"So, growing up, my old man fixed cars—or at least, that's what he called it. One morning, he found a dog hiding under the wheel of some broken-down junker." I shake my head, thinking about it. "My old man spotted it and called out, 'Well, ain't you sexy.'" I chuckle a little bit at the memory. "My ma hated it. Pops brought that dog inside, and until the day it died, he called that poor fucker Sexy. Whenever my mom pissed him off, my pops would yell, 'Come on, Sexy. Give Daddy a kiss.'" I shake my head. It was gross and ridiculous, just like my dad. "Ma especially hated when he'd fight with her, because then he'd really pour it on."

A smile finally spreads across Lacey's face. I smirk and tell her, "And the funniest part was the dog was a boy. Dad tortured Ma by smooching and loving on his 'sexy boy.'" I roll my eyes. "No shade to dudes into dudes. Love is love and all that shit, but Dad just did it to fuck with her."

Lacey looks me over, and a small giggle slips past her lips. Then she covers her mouth and starts cracking up. "I don't know what's funnier, hearing you say 'dudes into dudes' or imagining your dad asking Sexy for kisses."

She's laughing harder now, but it's not like she's finding my stories all that funny. It's like something releases inside her, and she laughs and laughs until suddenly something shifts and she's sobbing, tears rolling down her cheeks. Her shoulders shake, and she lowers her head, crying into her hands.

"Oh fuck. Lacey..." I go to her and hold her again, this time pressing her soft body hard against mine. I feel the shudders of her chest, the sadness that tightens her back and weakens her knees. Her weight is fully against me, and she's clutching me like she never wants to let go.

I stroke her hair and just let her cry. I can't say I've comforted a lot of women in the past. I'm more the cut-and-run type, but this is different. Lacey is different. I've never had to hold someone through some kind of wrong being done to them. I'm usually facing off against someone who's done me wrong. Or who I've screwed over—either accidentally or on purpose.

There's no judgment here. Nothing I did wrong here, nothing to feel bad about. Except, of course, that Lacey is hurting. But somehow her pain makes me want to come closer. I want to do what I can to ease this for her, even if all I can do is let her drench the front of my Tom fucking Ford shirt with tears.

I chuckle when I realize she's using a dress shirt that

probably costs more than a month's mortgage payment on this place as a tissue.

She lifts her head and peers at me through wet lashes. "I'm sorry," she says. "This is bullshit. I shouldn't be taking all this out on you."

"I don't mind," I say. "I was just wondering how many of those six Gs this shirt cost those fuckers."

Lacey gasps and wipes her face dry with her hands. She sniffles. "Eagle, that shirt... I Googled it after the tailor left."

I hold up a hand. "I don't even want to know."

She looks at me then, her face red and puffy from crying, her sleep shirt wrinkled and damp from tears. "Eagle." She whispers my name. "Why did you come here tonight? After what I did last night..."

I shake my head. I don't know why I came here. I don't know what I want to admit. I may never be good enough for a woman like Lacey.

I take a step back from her. The urge to be honest, to touch her, to tell her I don't know what I want but I'm drawn to her like a kid's drawn to candy. I feel stupid. I don't know what to say. I sure as fuck can't tell her the truth.

"I can go. I just wanted to—"

"Don't," she says, stepping close to me. Her nipples are hard again, and her eyes are blazing with intensity. The tears are gone, and she's licking her lips, bare of that siren-red lipstick. She's as raw as a person can be, and she's looking at me with an honesty that makes me feel exposed. "I want you here. I want you to stay."

I shove my hands into my overpriced pockets, not knowing what to say or do.

"I brought beer and pizza. I thought you might be hungry. You want some?"

"I want you," she says. "Just you. I don't care if it's complicated. I don't care about tomorrow and my job. Tonight...I just want you."

For a second, my guts tighten into knots. She doesn't care about tomorrow, and somehow that stings. I want her to want more from me than just one night. I want to be the kind of guy that she can picture a future with. I want to be enough for this woman, this woman who, for the last two years, I've watched work and dance, laugh, and kick some serious ass when it was called for. And now, she's offering me a part of her. She's offering me tonight.

I could hold out for more, but I'm not that guy. I know tomorrow isn't promised to anyone, and it sure as hell isn't promised to guys like me.

I shut down my brain and kick my heart to the goddamn curb. She's offering me tonight, and that's more than I even deserve.

CHAPTER 9
LACEY

"SIT." I point to the couch, and Eagle doesn't hesitate. I flip off the light switch, plunging the sunroom into darkness, but I leave the ceiling fan running.

He sits and looks at me with an expression that's guarded, and for a second, I hesitate. I mean, nothing much has changed since the other night except now we're alone. Through every shitty moment of tonight— through my humiliation and stress—Eagle was there. He was so caring and kind to me.

This may be a bad decision, but I'm damned sure it can't be my worst.

His thick legs are covered in the most luxurious navy-blue fabric I've ever seen, and I straddle his lap. He widens his eyes, but those beautiful blues stare through me, challenging me, asking me.

Is this what you want?

Are you sure?

He doesn't have to say the words. After last night, I'm sure he's feeling unsettled, but I want the chance to feel something good. To set aside the shit of the last few weeks, the last few months, and just give in to what I want.

Not what I have to do.

Not what I need to do.

What I *want* to do.

I trace my fingers along his sharp jaw, down the side of his neck and across the collar of the shirt that feels softer than the thousand-thread-count sheets at the Lantana.

He swallows hard but doesn't touch me. It's like he's waiting to see what I'll do, like he's giving me time to find my way.

I lick my lips and lower my face to his. I whisper against his slightly open mouth, "Eagle, I'm sorry about last night. Can I please have a second chance?"

I feel a groan deep in his chest, a masculine growl that tears past his lips, but he doesn't do or say anything.

"Eagle." I breathe light kisses along the bottom of his mouth, teasing him with the softness of my lips.

He groans again, and then I feel his hands on my hips. "Lacey." His voice is thick. "What do you want from me?"

I'm comfortable straddling his lap, my legs bent at the knees. I rock my hips a bit and feel the crotch of his tux.

"Kiss me," I whisper.

He doesn't miss a beat. He slides his hands beneath my hair and cups my neck, and then he draws my face toward his. He kisses my right eye, then my left, taps the tip of my nose with his, and flicks the tip of his tongue against my lower lip.

Then, he consumes me. My eyes fall closed as bliss floods my body at his kiss. Our mouths are open, tasting each other, kissing, licking, sucking. I'm wiggling against his erection; my sleep shorts already damp from how aroused I am.

His hands leave my hips and move to the front of my thin T-shirt. "This okay?" he asks. "We giving your neighbors a show?"

I giggle. "Fence," I breathe.

The fan whirs above us, and the moon shines bright in the dark sky as I feel Eagle cup my breasts in his hands. Through the fabric, he strokes my nipples with the pads of his thumbs, the friction sparking delicious pings that travel from my nipples to my core.

I lift my face from his, arching my back to give him more of my tits. I can't help what I'm doing now. My hips move on their own, driven by need and desire, dancing a rhythm against his lap that comes from some-place so primal, so instinctive, it just feels right.

Beneath my thighs, the gorgeous texture of the tuxedo pants caresses my skin as I move. Eagle lifts the hem of my sleep shirt and exposes my breasts, my nipples practically screaming with need when the air hits my skin. But then he sucks me into his mouth, and I go weak. I grip his shoulders, and a flood of arousal coats my pussy. Every pulse of his tongue over my hard tip sends another wave of need through me.

I grip his shoulders and rock against his cock. I press my chest into his face, frantic for more. I weave my fingers through the back of his hair, feeling his stubble under my fingertips and pressing his head lightly so he knows he can take all of me into his mouth.

He pants and suckles, drawing my whole nipple, my entire areola into his mouth. My breasts disappear in his large hands as he kneads me, tugs me, and pulls me deeper into his mouth.

"Eagle," I pant and whimper. My eyelids are so heavy, I feel like I'm looking at him through water, but I want to watch.

I've never dry humped another person before, but between his mouth on my breast, his cock straining against the pants beneath me, and the satiny tuxedo fabric stroking my inner thighs as I move, I nearly come undone.

"I might come," I whisper, hardly able to get the words out. "Eagle, fuck, I might…"

I arch my back, and suddenly, Eagle slows, pulling his mouth from me. My body immediately starts to cool, and I wonder if he's going to stop everything, cut me off at the last possible minute just like I did to him last night.

But I'm so wrong. He shifts his ass on the couch and wriggles a hand beneath him. He pulls out his wallet and drops it onto the cushion beside us.

"Condom?" he asks. "I've got two left."

I chuckle and shake my head. Since he's not planning on shoving me aside, I want to pay back the attention he's paid to me.

I slide off his lap, expecting to see a giant wet spot on the front of his pants, but I don't. Just a raging erection that looks like it's about to break through that pricey zipper.

I drop to my knees between Eagle's legs. "Is this okay?" I ask, slowly working down his zipper.

"Whatever you want, babe." His voice is thick, and I am not at all surprised to see he's wearing boxers with little motorcycles on them under his tux. The briefs are loose, and I'm able to slip my hands into the opening and gently tug his dick out. I don't know how comfortable this will be, but I want to suck him while he's still in the tux.

I kneel as close to the couch as I can and rub my palms along the tops of his thighs. Then I lean forward and kiss the head of his cock. Just a soft kiss, nothing wet or deep, but a shudder rocks Eagle's whole body at the contact.

I grin at the power my touch has on him, then take the length of him in my hands. His dick is hard and the skin soft. Thick veins run up the length of him, and I find a tiny tender spot under the head of his cock that is just begging to be licked. I lower my head, and I press a kiss to his tip.

He groans and slides his tattooed hands through my hair, tightening his fingers. "I don't wanna hurt you," he says. "You tell me if this is no good."

"Mmm," I hum, sucking his length in deep. I don't answer. It feels good. Everything about him feels hot and soft, hard and delicious. I wish I could see the rest of his body, the tattoos on his arms and the muscles I've gaped at for years, but we'll have time. I *hope* we'll have time.

Right now is just for him. Trying not to drench the front of his tux pants, I hold his shaft in one hand and suck him into my mouth. He works his fingers lightly through my hair, tugging and helping me set the right pace as I suck his dick. I swirl the tip of my tongue against the underside of his cock, feeling every tremble and gasp as I bring him to the edge.

"I wanna fuck you," he whispers, his voice a rasp.

I reluctantly pull my mouth from him and grab a foil packet from the couch cushion. I tear it open, pull out the latex, and roll it over his length. He doesn't move, doesn't try to take off his pants, and I love it.

What I have in mind is filthy and seductive and blows every fantasy I've had about this man out of the water.

Still wearing my sleep shorts, I straddle his lap again and move the material of my shorts to one side so I can take him inside me.

"You might not be able to sell the tux after this," I whisper.

He grunts a laugh, then says, "It might just become my new uniform if I know this happens when I wear it."

I laugh, but the sound dies in my throat as I rub the tip of his cock against my clit. I'm wet and swollen and so hot for him.

I want to fuck him, but I want to feel him first. I hold his cock in one hand and work my hips back and forth against his shaft, moaning and sighing with every exquisite stroke against my clit. I close my eyes and feel

Eagle cup my tits again, pinching my nipples between his fingers.

"No," I whisper, "Oh God, I don't want this to stop. I don't wanna come."

"Come for me, Lacey," Eagle says. "I want to watch you come apart."

My eyelids clamped shut, I shift my hips and settle my weight over Eagle's cock, then slide down on him inch by ever-loving precious inch. I'm almost coming before he's all the way inside me, but I clench my walls and sink down hard and fast.

"Fuck," he groans, and he drops his head back against the couch.

I ride him hard, fast, and dirty, the fabric of my loose sleep shorts wet and sticky with sweat and arousal. When I finally come, it washes over me like a tidal wave. I feel the climax building, building, but then it's happening. His hands are gripping my breasts, and the pleasure is so intense, I don't ever want it to stop. I'm riding him, trying not to scream into the silence of the night.

I drop my mouth to his and moan. "More, more," I demand. "Don't stop fucking me."

And it's true. The waves of pleasure keep hitting me, like I've been dunked underwater and there is no way I'll find the surface.

My legs start to burn from the effort of riding him, my nipples are tender and sore, but even though he is quiet, cursing and tugging on my hips like he might fuck his way right through my shorts, he doesn't make anything more than a few desperate moans.

When he slows, I collapse onto his shoulder and just breathe. Breathe in the light scent of soap and expensive material. The breaths that we share as our chests rise and fall in time together.

After what seems like forever, locked together and unmoving, I lift my head. I meet his eyes, and his face looks guarded and spent. Like's he's tired but braced for bad news.

"Eagle," I whisper, "do you think the pizza is cold?"

He barks a laugh, and everything about his body relaxes. "Don't matter to me, babe," he says. "You need fuel?"

I nod, reluctantly sliding off his lap. I carefully peel the condom from him, trying to keep the mess inside the latex. I adjust my shorts to cover myself and walk over to the table. There are no napkins or anything, so I hold up a finger to him and slip quietly inside the house.

When I get back to the sunroom, Eagle's shirt is unbuttoned halfway, and his pants are zipped. He's opened two beers and is drinking one.

"You want water?" I ask.

He shakes his head and hands me a beer. The can is cold enough, so I grab a slice of pizza and motion for him to do the same. He does, and then we sit side by side on the couch, the whir of the ceiling fan tossing the air over our cooling bodies.

"You can stay," I tell him. "I mean, sleep here with me, if you want. I'll wake you up in time to get back to the Lantana in the morning."

"I am not going to the Lantana," he says quietly. "I got a friend to cover my shift. Carla okayed it."

I stop chewing and look up at him cautiously. "But why? Don't you need the money? Why wouldn't you go back there?"

Eagle takes a long pull on his beer before looking me in the eyes. "Let's just say after what those assholes did to you, I wouldn't exactly be the best guy to stop trouble if it started tomorrow. I might even be the one to start it if the wrong buttons got pushed."

"What they did to me?" I ask softly.

This is not a conversation I want to have now. This is not a conversation I ever really want to have. I'm the one in the wrong in the situation, though. What did the Acostas do other than find out the truth at the worst possible time?

"I don't know what happened, and I don't care," Eagle says quietly, wiping his mouth with a paper towel. "Those people are fake and they're assholes. I'll live without a half day's pay."

I look down at my pizza, the cheese a little thick now that it's cool, but damn, it still tastes delicious. Too bad I don't have much of an appetite now.

"I am so sorry."

He reaches for my chin and presses his index finger against my lips. "I liked it better when you were talking about how fuckable I am in this tux."

I nod, relieved in a way that he doesn't want to know. Maybe he does, or will at some point, but right now, I want to feel good and enjoy whatever this moment is with Eagle. Because things are going to look very, very different in my life, come Monday. I'll be explaining a lot of my story to a lot of people. I don't really want to talk about it, and thankfully, Eagle doesn't seem to need me to.

"What about your mom?" Eagle asks. "She gonna mind waking up on Sunday morning to a strange man in her house?"

I shake my head and point at my wrist. I'm not wearing a watch, but I should check the time. "She leaves at the crack of dawn for work. She manages PM bakery."

Eagle's quiet for a minute, then he says, "Best damn cinnamon raisin bread at PM. Your ma works there?"

I nod, a little proud that something about a basic grocery store job doesn't seem basic to Eagle. I never even told Dylan the name of the store where my mom worked. He didn't seem to have any interest at all. "I mean, that's not her recipe, but…" I grin. "We have like three loaves in the freezer. I can make you toast for breakfast."

He stands up from the cushion and grabs my hand. "Let's get out of these clothes," he says, lifting his brows at me. "Unless you really want me to sleep in the suit. For you, I'd consider it."

CHAPTER 10
EAGLE

I STIR when I hear Lacey talking softly, but that's not what wakes me up. After spending a couple of hours beside Lacey, her bare legs tucked into mine, my arm thrown over her, the sudden loss of her warmth against my naked body jolts me like a bucket of water to the face.

She is speaking softly into her phone and tapping quietly at the keyboard of an old-looking laptop. "Okay," she says. "No. No, don't do that."

She's tapping her bare toes against the floor as she glares at the monitor. "We prepared a gluten-free and a dairy-free option," she says. "Are you telling me the bride wants to make a major change to the menu three hours before the meal is supposed to be served?"

Lacey covers her face with one hand and sighs. "I'm sorry, Carla. I know. I'm sorry. That's not what happened at all. All you need to do is show them this. I'm sending the final menu that was initialed and signed by both the bride and groom weeks ago when we took the final guest tally."

I scratch the sleep from my eyes and grab my phone. It's nine, and no doubt the Asshat Family is giving Carla some trouble on their last morning. I roll over onto my side and tuck a pillow under my head, adjusting my view so I can watch Lacey work.

She notices me tossing around in bed and throws me a smile, but then mouths, "Sorry, almost done."

Then she's back to business.

"There *is* a price difference," Lacey snaps, not snapping at Carla. "So, you can just tell the bride that the plated meals require not only a different *preparation* but a different *presentation*. She ordered a brunch buffet, and she's getting a brunch buffet."

Lacey holds up a "wait" finger to me and then puts the phone on speaker. Carla is talking a mile a minute and sounds like she's been crying already.

Jesus.

"…and then she told me that it didn't matter what Lacey sold them, because, as far as she knew, Lacey was fired…"

My heart drops at that. Lacey was most certainly not fired, and she corrects Carla immediately.

"Carla, I was *not* fired," she says, slamming down the lid of her laptop and coming back to bed. "Due to some issues that I had with the Acostas, Don made the decision to do whatever it took to keep the peace at the wedding."

"But Lacey, they're saying they want all these

changes..." Carla sounds frazzled, and I feel bad for the kid.

I hold up a finger, and Lacey mutes the phone.

"Remind her that Brute and Arrow are there to protect her too." I lower one brow and shake my head, firing off a text to Arrow and Brute to keep an eye on the wedding planner.

Lacey looks grateful and mouths thank you, and then she unmutes the phone. "Carla, I can't come in today, but I need you to bring in Don or whoever is on today... Okay, fine, good. Don was there last night. He made the decision to send me home; he should be the one to explain to the Acostas that we can't change the breakfast buffet at the last minute. Loop him in, and don't forget to call in the security guys if they give you any real trouble... I know, Carla. I know. I'm sorry. You're doing a great job. I know you are. I know you. You never do anything less than your best, okay? Okay. All right. Go ahead. Good, then. Tell Arrow thank you for me. Okay. I'll see you tomorrow, Carla. Bye."

Lacey hangs up the call and drops down on the side of the bed. "Your friends work fast," she says, a sad smile on her face.

"Arrow?" I guess.

She nods. "Did you text him? He showed up like a ghost while I was talking with her. He offered to talk to the Acostas with Carla. He might also have offered to do some damage to the man if needed."

I chuckle. "Arrow's good people. He'll take care of her."

Lacey nods, but that smile turns from sad to

thoughtful. "They're telling people I was fired," she says quietly. "But I'm not…at least not yet."

I stroke her back through the thin sleep shirt and then tug on it slightly. "Today," I tell her, "is your day off. You can let Carla worry about the shit at work, and you can worry about nothing. How about that? Let's make this a day you worry about nothing."

She nods and leans back against my chest. "I love the sound of that. Do you want to come with me to pick up Ruby?" She turns and faces me. "Unless you have things you have to do today. I can just make you breakfast really quick if you need to go."

I wrap my arms around her and tug her back toward me. "Babe, I was supposed to work today. I got no place else I'd rather be."

She lifts her face and kisses me lightly, a smile returning to her face. "Cinnamon raisin toast? I can make French toast with it if you want that instead?"

I shake my head. "The only breakfast I want is right here in this bed. I have one condom left, and it's gotta be lonely in my wallet."

The small smile spreads, and before I know it, she's tugging the sleep shirt over her head.

———

I insist on driving her to get Ruby. I know it might seem stupid, but now that I've got her, I don't want to let her go. There's nothing calling me back to the compound except a clean pair of pants, which I figure I can stop and get later.

I take a shower at Lacey's so I don't stink like sex. Although once I put on the tuxedo pants from last night and remember what we did to them, I'm pretty sure that everything I'm wearing definitely smells like sex.

After we fuck again, eat, shower, and dress, we climb into my truck and head for the dog.

I don't know why I didn't realize it sooner. The kennel is none other than the Canine Crashpad, the business owned by Leo's old lady and Tiny's kid. Lia told Lacey to come in around noon, and when we hit the parking lot, I see two motorcycles I recognize right up front.

The strip mall where the doggie day care is located is a small industrial-looking plaza with an auto service station on the far end. There is a vacant office space where Arrow used to rent a place for his business and an office that the VP of the club and his wife use to manage the property-related business. They bought this strip mall a couple years back when the club went clean.

Now, Morris runs a small property management company, and he's got his fingers in construction projects and other businesses. Just about every one of us works in some way or at some time in some aspect of the legit businesses.

All except me.

I've spent the last couple years drifting, doing my own thing. That's how I happened on the security gig at the Lantana. I didn't want to haul debris and wear a hard hat, show up at a jobsite before dawn, even if that meant working with my brothers.

If I had an old lady like Morris, and even more so if I had a kid at home, you couldn't get me to work on Sunday unless it was for overtime and something I felt like doing. I feel like a hypocrite even thinking it, though. How many Sundays have I worked for regular-time pay at the Lantana over the last two years? Just because the job wasn't what everyone else would do, because it was my choice.

Maybe that's the reason. Or maybe the reason is sitting right here beside me in the passenger seat of my truck.

I climb out of the cab and go around to open Lacey's door, but she's already bouncing out, looking excited. She grins at me, and I wonder if I should take her hand or what the right thing to do is here, but she rushes past me, heading full steam for the front door of the Canine Crashpad.

Lacey's wearing a pair of very short denim shorts that show enough of her ass to keep me on the verge of a chubby, sandals with a little heel, and a tiny T-shirt that exposes her soft belly whenever she moves her arms. Her hair is loose, and she's wearing no makeup, sunglasses pushed up on her head, looking free and relaxed.

"I see her," Lacey squeals, clapping her hands and pointing through the locked glass door.

I see people I know too, so I point through the glass, but at a very different target.

Lia comes rushing toward the door, looking like an ad for a music festival. She's wearing this super-short off-white crocheted dress and leather flip-flops, her long brown hair tied back in a floral scarf.

"Welcome back, Mama." Lia opens the door and motions for Lacey to come inside.

My heart skips a beat for a second when she calls Lacey Mama, but then I realize Lia's referring to the dog, not a human baby.

"Look what a good girl she was." Lia bends down and scratches a large, short-haired, brown-and-black German shepherd behind the ears.

The dog flops down on her side and kicks one foot in the air, basically choosing Lia's pets over a joyful reunion with her mom.

Lacey shakes her head. "Well, I can see I wasn't missed." She drops down on her knees and vigorously rubs Ruby's belly while thanking Lia for coming in early.

Lia walks up to me and smacks me on the shoulder. "Eagle, who knew? You clean up nice," She follows up the smack with a big hug, then leans into my ear, fake-coughs, then whispers so loudly I am sure Lacey hears every word, "Walk of shame much?"

I hug her back, shaking my head. "A gentleman doesn't kiss and tell, but I ain't no gentleman." I laugh. "Still, I'm not answering."

"Oh, come on." Lia claps her hands. "Tell me I'm the first to know. Is there anything to know? What's the story?"

Her excitement for the fact that I look like I fucked Lacey last night is cut off when Tiny emerges from the back of the day care.

"If Eagle got laid, I don't wanna hear it." Tiny's name is pure irony, because he is the total opposite. He lost a little weight last year, but on a man his size, the little bit he lost isn't much. He seems committed to being healthier, even working out with Leo, Lia's husband, once in a while on the equipment we have at the club.

I clap him on the shoulder. "What the fuck you doing here on a Sunday?" I ask.

Tiny jerks a thumb toward the back. "Had to take a shit. Went for a ride with Morris, and this place was closer than going all the way back to the compound."

"Dad." Lia grimaces. "Please tell me you flushed. I don't want to have to have the talk again."

"We ain't talking about anything having to do with my shit," Tiny confirms. "So, don't ask." He leans forward and kisses his daughter on the cheek, then points to my tux. "Speaking of shit. You liked that crap so much you're still wearing it?"

I shake my head and point to Lacey. "Tiny, this is Lacey. She is my boss over at the Lantana."

Tiny extends a hand to shake Lacey's and seems to put two and two together without my painting a more vivid picture than that.

"Nice to meet you, Lacey." He points to me. "Watch out for this one. He's a dickhead, through and through." He cackles when he says it, but I notice Lacey's smile lose a little bit of its luster.

"All right, fuck off," I say, nodding at Tiny.

As soon as Lacey stands and stops petting Ruby, the dog leaps to her feet as if she's just noticed me. She immediately smashes her nose into my crotch and starts sniffing like she's trying to figure out how the hell she smells Lacey all over my junk.

Since Lia's busy at the tablet at the front desk, I let the dog sniff. Probably the best way to get her to trust me is to let her smell her mama all over me. I hold out the back of my hand, fingers cupped down, and let the Shepherd sniff me. Finally, she lets me pet her, and then she leans into it.

Tiny throws a wave up behind him and heads out to the parking lot. Lacey signs the checkout form confirming she picked up her dog and gives Lia a hug. "Thank you. Ruby loves it here. She doesn't look like she's in any rush to go home."

Lia and Lacey turn and watch me loving on Ruby. I clear my throat. "We good?" I ask.

Just then, my phone buzzes with a text message. I grab the phone from my pocket, assuming it has to be Arrow with a question about the brunch. I swipe the lock screen to check the message, but it's not from Arrow.

Linda: We need to talk. You around today?

Fuck.

She doesn't say more than that, but Linda only texts me when she wants something or wants to say something to piss me off. Sometimes I think she does that just for kicks.

I can't decide whether to tell her to go fuck herself or just to ignore the text. Now isn't a good time for either pissing off Linda or talking to her, and basically, no matter what I do, it won't be the right thing. She always finds a way to make a federal fucking case out of everything and anything. And if she can make me feel stupid or shitty in the process, it's just a bigger win.

I want to ignore her, but if I don't reply, she'll start calling.

Lacey has Ruby on her leash and is headed toward me. "Ready?" she asks.

I don't know if she's seen me look at my phone or if she cares either way. But something about Linda texting me while I'm with Lacey makes my stomach churn.

I flip the slider to silence my phone. This is my time with Lacey, and come hell or high water—and knowing Linda, it's likely gonna be both—she's going to have to wait.

CHAPTER 11
LACEY

BY THE TIME we get back to my house, Mom is home from work. Eagle slows to a stop in front and seems to notice the faint light from the TV visible through the vertical blinds.

"Am I dropping you here?" he asks, nodding at the house.

Ruby jumps up from the back seat, excited to be home. I don't know what to say to Eagle. He's still in the tux from last night, so if I invite him in, Mom won't have any choice but to think about why he's dolled up in extremely wrinkled formalwear on a Sunday afternoon.

"My mom's home," I say, not sure how he'll react. "Do you want to meet her?" I don't know whether I want him to say yes or no. If this were just any other day, not a day when I should be working but was sent home, then Eagle wouldn't be here. He wouldn't still be wearing his tux. But I'm a grown woman, and despite all the shit decisions I've made when it comes to men, I know my mom will be sweet to him.

Eagle seems to study my face, looking for clues about how to answer.

I hesitate a second. My mom hasn't met many of the men I've dated, and I don't even know if what this is, this thing I've done with Eagle, will last beyond today.

While I'm waiting for his answer, Eagle looks down at his phone. It's in the cupholder facing him so I can't see it, but it looks like he's seeing something pop up on it now. He thins his lips and says, "Maybe I'm a gentleman after all." He kills the truck engine and unfastens his seat belt. "You don't mind if I walk you to the door? Maybe she won't notice the tux."

He smiles, and all I see are the crinkles around his eyes, the blue as he grins, lighting up the car and matching the brilliant afternoon sky. My heart flips a little in my chest, and my core quivers a little. I don't want to say goodbye to him. For the first time in a long time, I wish I had my own place. Wish I had privacy to drag his sexy ass and his sunshine smile right back into my bedroom for a marathon Sunday of sex.

But I live in reality, and that means I live with Mom. Whatever happens with Eagle, it has to happen under Mom's roof.

Eagle picks up his phone, and I can't tell if he means it or if he's coming up with a convenient excuse.

"You know what, some asshole's blowing up my phone. I need to grab this." He leans across the console and takes my chin in his hand. "You know how to find me," he says. Then he pulls me close, plants a light kiss on my lips, and puts his seat belt back on.

My heart sinks.

I feel so stupid. I should beg him to come in, invite him in for coffee or lunch, but he's already swiping on his phone, his brows lowered.

"Thanks," I say quietly. "For everything."

I don't think I sound sincere, but I don't know what to sound like. I unfasten my seat belt, jump out of the car, and push the passenger seat back so Ruby can jump down from the back seat. I adjust the seat back to where it belongs, close the passenger door, and grip Ruby's leash in my hands.

I look up at Eagle through the closed windows, worrying my lower lip between my teeth. He looks at me before he drives away, but I can't read his expression.

I can't fixate on it. It's none of my business. I lead Ruby toward the front door.

"Ruby." My mom's voice echoes over the excited scratching of claws against the kitchen tile. "You're home early."

I kick off my sandals and head into the kitchen, feeling lower than I can believe. I feel like I did something wrong. Like everything is off between Eagle and me, and I don't even know what everything is. All I know is things feel weird, and I don't even know why.

"You okay, baby?" Mom's got her hands in the sink. "You feel like barbecuing?"

I come up behind my mom, her strong, slender body smelling like coconut vanilla, her favorite shower gel.

And my all-time favorite scent, because it's hers. I rest my head against the back of Mom's shoulder and sigh. "Sounds delish," I say. "Can I cook?"

"I'd love it," Mom says. She nods toward the fridge. "Honey, did you order a pizza last night? There's almost a whole uneaten pizza in the fridge. I was going to steal a slice for lunch, but then I thought maybe I shouldn't since I don't know when you bought it or why."

If I thought I was going to be able to hide the fact that Eagle was here from Mom, I wasn't thinking that one through.

"I didn't, but one of the guys from work did," I explain. "He stopped over late last night to talk about everything that happened."

Mom tosses me a look over her shoulder, using the back of her raw chicken hand to turn on the cold water. "Late? How late, baby? I didn't hear anything."

I smother a grin, relieved she didn't hear.

"It was very late," I admit. "He came after the wedding ended."

My mom is quiet, and I'm not sure if she's busy with the chicken or lost in thought. I reach around her to fill Ruby's empty water dish with cold water and give my mom a look.

"You got quiet," I say. "Are you okay?"

She nods. "I'm fine. Are you, though? What happened at work was a lot."

She looks at me, her lips thin. My mother had me when she was nineteen years old. Just a kid having a baby and doing it all alone. Some people with young parents feel like they grew up with their parents, but I never felt that way. My mom always acted like the adult. She never saddled me with worries that she knew I shouldn't have to handle.

We've had rough times, but through it all, she's always believed in me, seen me, and cared about me. She's never once judged me for my shitty taste in men or my career choices. She didn't have the money to pay for college, but she cosigned for my student loans.

She's done everything she could to give me an amazing life. She knows me better than anyone in the world does, and right now, she knows just the right thing to say. Rather than judge me for having a man over in the middle of the night, she knows that yesterday had to be hard for me.

I sniffle and shrug. "It was a lot, but what can I do? The thing that happened with Dylan happened. Maybe I made the wrong call not disclosing the relationship to the Lantana. They could have trained Carla to run the event in my place. I should have known that somebody would end up making a scene at that wedding. I just always assumed it would be me or him."

Mom pats the hen dry with a paper towel, then frowns. "I don't think I would have told my boss. I mean, Lacey, come on. It's none of their business who you date in your private life. Is there a policy against that? Do you have an employment contract or a handbook?"

I shake my head. "We have a handbook that discourages any behavior that could lead the Lantana into any situation that could present a conflict of inter-est, but that's pretty vague."

"Not to mention broad," Mom agrees. "Look," she says, setting the chicken out and scrubbing her hands clean. "They don't own you. You were caught up in a situation you had no control over. A different man would have handled his daughter's wedding with class, Lacey. This man chose how the situation was going to play out. Just like he chose the way your rela-tionship was going to play out."

My face burns with shame, but I know my mom's not throwing shade at me. We've talked about Dylan many times, and Mom has always been adamant. In case I forgot how she feels, she tells me again.

"You were lied to, Lacey. You assumed the man you were dating was available to date you. It's not your fault that he's married." Mom dries her hands and opens a cabinet, banging around for the spices to make a marinade. "This is all on him."

As many times as Mom says it, I cannot help myself. I can't agree with her. It was not all on him. I wasn't suspicious enough, jealous enough, demanding enough. I tried so hard to be easy, to be low-key. To be a woman who wouldn't put demands on him or force him into a box, and instead, I gave him enough rope to hang me with.

I should never have been so trusting or naïve. Dylan did all the lying, but I do feel responsible for my part in believing the lies. I made it easy for him.

"Thanks, Mom," I say, standing from the table and grabbing hot sauce and limes from the fridge. I set them down for her next to the spices and oils she's missing, then lean on my elbow and watch her.

I know that what happened isn't my fault, and yet I feel guilt. I thought a broken heart was the worst of the consequences I'd suffer, but I know better now. It takes two to tango, and Dylan dances dirty.

"So," Mom says, her voice brighter. "Who's the pizza and beer guy?"

I smile, feeling a comfortable warmth replace the burning feelings of shame. "One of the security guards at the Lantana," I explain. "He's really interesting."

My mom barks out a laugh. "Interesting? He must be very, very interesting if you invited him to your mother's house in the middle of the night."

"Mom." I shake my head.

"You're a grown woman," she says, holding up a hand. She's got a whisk in her hand and sets to work mixing up her famous chicken marinade. "I just hope…" she says quietly, then trails off.

I'm still leaning on the counter like I'm fifteen and not thirty, like the hardest decision we have to make is how much to let me spend on my new school backpack.

"Hope what, Mom?"

She looks into my eyes then, hers a light gray to my chocolate brown. Mom exhales a long, slow breath. "Just what I always hope, Lacey. That he deserves you."

I hope that too. I'm tired of all the disappointing men. Guys like my dad who run at the first sign of trouble, or men like Dylan who want only what they want and will do anything it takes to get what they want, and when they finally do get it, they leave.

I've never met my dad. I don't even know much about him except that he told my mom he didn't want to be a dad, didn't want a relationship, and took off before Mom was barely six months along. Sometimes I wonder if he even knows I was born.

It may sound wild, but I've never Googled him, never looked him up. I've been tempted many times, but in truth, I'm afraid to. If my father has a wife and three beautiful kids, I don't want to know about it. To see him living the fantasy with someone else would kill me.

Instead, I try not to think about him. I try not to wonder or question. Like so many men in my life since my dad, reality can be so much worse than the fantasy.

That unsettled feeling I had when Eagle left comes over me again. I don't know what he deserves—or even what I deserve. What he is or who he is. Maybe he's a guy who has a kid out there, or he could be like me, stuck in a holding pattern.

Maybe it's too soon for me to be thinking this way, but I can't help agreeing with my mom. I have a feeling I like Eagle, and I only hope he's not going to shatter my heart.

CHAPTER 12
EAGLE

WHEN I GET BACK to the compound, I don't even get out of my truck before calling Linda back. I don't need an audience for this conversation.

"What's up?" I say, leaning back in my seat.

"I've been trying to reach you all damn day, Eagle." She isn't saying anything that I need to respond to, but I can't help but put her in her place.

"And I've had shit to do, Linda, so why don't you stop trying to fuck with me and tell me what you want," I say, wanting her to cut to the fucking chase.

"You know, Eagle, you're a dick."

"Heard it before, and I'll hear it again," I say. "So, why don't you tell me something I don't know. Like what you want from me now?"

"What I want from you now? I literally never fucking bother you, Eagle, and I actually do need something, and you're giving me this shit?"

"Okay," I say, unfastening my seat belt. "This is going nowhere, and I've got places to be—"

"Eagle, wait." Linda's composed now, which sets off alarm bells in my head. She wants something. Between her insistent efforts to reach me and the sudden shift in tone, I'm in for it.

"What?" I demand. "What do you want?"

Linda takes a long, slow breath. I can hear her trying to steady herself, so I stop this line of thought before it goes any further.

"No," I say. "Unless something's changed on your end, no."

Linda curses quietly into the phone. "Eagle," she says, her voice dripping with anger. "I need that divorce. I want it. So let's just move ahead and do this."

"Are you willing to budge?" I ask. "Are you calling to tell me you've changed your mind?"

Linda is a little more measured, a little less enraged. "No," she says, her smoker's voice still angry, still mean. "You're the one who pushed me into marrying you…"

We've been through this story a hundred fucking thousand times. No, I did not push Linda into marrying me. When we thought she was pregnant, I offered to do the right thing. That was the last right thing that happened between us.

"Linda, I'm not doing this. I'm hanging up now. Unless you've changed your mind, I'm not divorcing you."

"Fuck you, Eagle, you're a—"

I have no problem ending the call while she's talking. I just wish these damn cell phones had a more satisfying smashing sound. I hung up on Linda plenty in the days when we still had a landline at the compound. It may be petty, but before I hang up on her, I press the star key and hold it down so she gets a nice buzzing sound in her ear right before I hang up.

As soon as the call ends, I feel like an asshole. A petty, malicious asshole. I could have just hung up on her, but somehow treating Linda like shit doesn't land the same as it usually does. I'm either getting soft or—and this is the more likely reality—I'm getting soft on someone else. Someone who makes me want to feel good, not bad. Someone whose texts and calls I want to see, not someone who boils my blood just by being in my contact list.

I climb out of the truck, desperate for a change of clothes and a decent meal. I wander into the compound and find Brute already home from the brunch.

"Yo, asshole. Nice clothes. Why the fuck you still wearing them?" He's grabbing a beer from the fridge, the dress shirt and pants he wore to brunch at the Lantana already gone, replaced by a frayed Slayer T-shirt and broken-in black jeans.

I follow him to the fridge and grab a beer for myself. "Fuck off."

I pop the cap and take a long swig of the cold beer. The bubbles fizz in my mouth and remind me of drinking warmish beer in the sun-room with Lacey.

"Dude, did you bang the wedding planner? Is that why you wanted Arrow to swap in for you today?" Brute asks.

"Fuck off," I tell him again. "I got old lady problems, man. Linda's on my ass again."

Brute nods. "Fuck that bitch."

I hold up the bottle of my beer, and we tip the necks together in a toast. "Fuck Linda."

Everyone in the club knows the deal with Linda. There's a long and dirty history between us, and if Linda could just let me loose and not try to fuck with me, my marriage would be over on paper, not just in reality. Not that we ever had a "real" marriage. I think we were legal all of two months when Linda, relieved maybe that she wasn't knocked up thanks to my carelessness, started hanging around with a rival club and whoring herself out to anyone with a lap and a boner.

She was unfaithful from the get, and rather than let my heart get crushed time and time again, I did my own thing too. We haven't lived as husband and wife in over twenty years, but that doesn't keep her from trying to make me miserable every chance she gets.

With a new topic to pick on, Brute slams my old lady a few more times, and I pile on too. She is a bitch, and she deserves every bit of trash we talk about her. If she changes the way she treats me, I'll leave her alone. Set her free and never look back. But as long as she keeps pulling shit, she's nothing to me and deserves as much.

"Speaking of bitches," I ask, pivoting again. "How was the rest of the wedding?"

"That family..." Brute shakes his head. "Fuck 'em, man. That mother of the bride made Lacey's replacement—what's her name?"

"Carla."

"Carla, yeah. They made her cry like three times today."

I roll my eyes. Not surprising, but I'm sorry Carla had to be on the receiving end of their shit. "Figures. Arrow do okay?"

Brute nods. "Arrow's straight, man. He did good."

We shoot the shit a little more, and then I ask when he's seeing Crow next.

"Tuesday," Brute confirms. "I'm off tomorrow. I need some sleep and about a thousand beers."

He wanders off to his room, and I go to mine, stripping out of the tux. I head off to the shower. I'm gonna make it a cold one because I'm still not over Lacey.

———

By the time I get out of the shower, I have four texts from Linda. I read and delete each one since none of them says anything new.

But then I get a text from Lacey and my heart starts thumping harder in my chest.

It's ridiculous. I'm like a teenager again, breathless and wondering what the girl I like has to say. I'm an idiot, and I brace myself for the "That was fun, but..." or "Last night was an accident" text.

I force myself to read it once, then a second time. It doesn't say what I think it's going to say. She's not blowing me off, brushing me aside, or acting like what happened didn't happen.

She's inviting me over for dinner.

Lacey: My mom's marinating chicken, and I'm planning on grilling. Want to join us for dinner?

She's not just inviting me over for dinner. She's inviting me over for dinner with her mother.

My fingers freeze, and my mind starts to work overtime.

Lacey is my sun, has been for a long time before I even realized she fit into that space. I gravitate toward her like a planet, pulled by a force that's powerful, and yet somehow, I never understood it. I still don't see it for what it is, but I can't care. I know how I feel. I know what I want. Even if it's only one more afternoon, one chill barbecue chicken dinner with her mom, I want it. I'll take every minute and morsel Lacey will give me.

Me: Can I bring anything?

It's a minute or so before Lacey replies with a time and asks if I know her address.

Me: Still got it

Lacey: Maybe bring condoms?

I chuckle and shake my head.

Lacey: Mom's talking about seeing an early movie with a girlfriend, so…

Me: Looking forward to it.

Since I'm already showered, I've got a couple hours to kill before I head back to Lacey's for dinner. Plenty of time to make a stop. No gentleman goes to a woman's house for dinner without bringing something. Maybe that fucking suit has changed me after all.

CHAPTER 13
LACEY

I'M STUPIDLY nervous about Eagle coming to dinner. He said yes, which maybe means that our hookup could lead to... I don't know, but I'm buzzing with excitement.

"But what's his name?" My mom looks confused.

"Just call him Eagle," I say, realizing that to my straitlaced Mom, telling her that I invited over my work friend who is a biker probably sounds the same as if I said call him by his street name, his mobster name, or his gang name.

Are those even things? I mean, how would we know? The closest I've ever been to a motorcycle is drooling over the guys on one of my favorite television shows. Mom and I watched that entire series together, and it's like she's putting the pieces together in her mind.

"Honey," she says, "I'll call him Peter Pan if that's what he prefers, but..." She's tossing a big green salad with sliced tomatoes in the kitchen, while I check the timer I set, so I know how long I have before I have to turn the chicken. "Is he…dangerous?"

I have to admit, I honestly don't know. I mean, I don't think so. He passed a background check for the Lantana, and while we don't run them again after someone is hired, he had to be clean, at least on paper, if he got the okay to be hired.

I tell her that, but I don't think that's what she means.

"Honey, don't bikers have a reputation for treating women a certain way?" she asks. "I mean, sleeping around, lying, drugs. How well do you know him?"

I have to admit, she's right. I don't know him well at all, and yet, I thought I knew Dylan.

"Mama," I say, using my pet name for her. "I like him. He's a friend. Maybe more. I'll find all this out before I get in too deep."

Mom nods, and I know she's just looking out for me. She cares, and her affection rarely comes with strings attached.

"I dated a biker once," she admits, her voice low. "It was a long time ago, right after your father."

"What?"

My mom never talks much about her dating life. I know she's had a few dates over the years, but like me, no one that really stuck.

She nods. "Just promise me you'll always wear a helmet," she says, growing serious. "Lacey Elizabeth Mercer, promise me right now."

I laugh and silence the timer on the chicken. "Mama,

I'm thirty years old! You can't use my middle name and scare me."

I hold up a finger and call out, "Chicken." Then I run to the grill to turn the meat. We ended up picking up two extra chickens so we have four cooking, but we didn't want to grill them whole, so I've got a lot of small pieces to turn.

When I head back inside, my mom's friend Danielle is helping herself to one of the beers Eagle brought yesterday. "You never buy this kind," she says, taking a sip. "Hmmm, I like it, though."

Mom dries her hands and gives Danielle a hug, then points to me. "Lacey's boyfriend brought that brand."

Danielle practically spits the beer from her mouth. "Oh my God. I'm sorry," she sputters. "I didn't even think to ask if this is fair game."

I wave my hand. "It's fine. He brought it for me, and I'm happy to share it."

I give Danielle a hug, and Mom takes the three-bean salad she brought and makes space for it in the fridge.

I start chopping up the potatoes for potato salad while Danielle grills me.

"So, are you back together with Dylan?" she asks gently, treading carefully over that prickly topic. "Or is this someone new?"

"Someone new," I say, grinning. "Not Dylan, thank God."

"He's a biker," my mom says, sounding awestruck. "Like, with a biker name and everything."

"Oh, stop." I wave a hand at my mother, who's

giving Danielle a look. "It's not like it looks on television. At least, I don't think so?"

Danielle raises an eyebrow. "Those guys are hot, Lace. Is he…" She makes a gesture with her hands that has Mom and me dying with laughter.

"I don't know what that means," I say. "But you can judge for yourself. He's coming over for dinner."

Danielle practically swoons and fans herself with her bare hand. "He's hot," she says. "I can just tell by your reaction. He's smoking hot."

I shake my head and run back to the chicken, my alarm ringing to remind me to baste. While I'm out back fussing over the grill, the doorbell must ring, because I hear Ruby barking like the world is coming to an end.

I rush inside, but Mom has already let Eagle in. He's carrying two bouquets of flowers and at least no condoms that are visible.

"Thank you. That was so thoughtful." My mom is beaming, and she takes the larger of the two bouquets that Eagle has extended to her.

He holds the second one in his hands. "Lacey." He nods when he sees me, and just like when I saw him in the tux for the first time, my heart catches in my chest and the rest of my body speeds up. It's almost dizzying the effect he has on me. It's as if the world around us collapses until all that's left is a tunnel that leads straight to him. To his bright-blue eyes, his sexy smile.

Today, he's wearing another gray T-shirt and the leather vest with his name on it. The sunglasses are already on his head, and his heavy boots sound against the floors with every step.

"Hi," I say to him, suddenly shy and excited and wishing I could fling myself into his arms. I take the flowers from him, cocking my chin at him. "Thank you." I open my arms, hoping he'll be okay with a hug.

He's more than okay with it. He draws me close to his chest and hugs me tight, the contact sending ripples of excitement down my spine. I hold him and breathe in the smell of him. I almost hum against him, I'm so happy to see and smell and touch him.

"Thanks for having me," he says. Then, noticing Danielle, he releases me and extends a hand. "I'm Eagle," he says. "My real name is a state secret, so Eagle'll do."

Danielle's face goes from stunned and silent to giggly and all grins. "Okay," she says. "I'm Danielle. Just Danielle."

They shake hands, and then Eagle turns to me, offering to help with anything we need. Meanwhile, I miss the question because Danielle has cupped her lips, but I can clearly see her mouth, "Oh my God," to my mother.

I shake my head, a little proud that, yeah, Eagle is hot. And he's here for me. I set the flowers in water and motion for him to join me outside. I go over to the grill, check the temperature of the hens, and then turn off the heat.

"We're almost ready," I say.

He's just standing there, though. His boots are planted in the grass, and the slightest hint of a breeze blows the tiny hairs on the back of my neck. I'm hot and flushed from the heat and humidity, but something about the way he's looking at me makes me *hot-hot*.

"Eagle?" I ask, stepping close to him.

"I want to kiss you so badly," he says, his voice low. "How much can Mom and Danielle take?"

I chuckle. "I promise I'll make it up to you." I check my smartwatch for the time. "That's why we're eating so early. They are trying to make the five o'clock show. Mom needs to be home and in bed by nine."

I watch his biceps flex as he extends a hand toward the grill. "Let's fucking eat, then." The corners of his mouth curl up, and I put the chicken on a clean plate and hand it to him to take back into the house.

We eat inside at the table, and Mom and Danielle are such old friends, they don't even have to press Eagle for information. We have music playing through the TV, and every once in a while, Danielle uses her spoon as a microphone and sings to the music, or Mom will get up from the table to refill someone's water and she'll shimmy along with the beat. Mom and Danielle keep the laughter going, and at times, they seem completely oblivious to the fact that we have a guest.

I don't think Eagle minds, and I sure don't. It's nice to be able to have things feel normal and yet have him here. I don't have to try too hard, although I do cringe when Mom and Danielle's favorite song comes on, and they pressure me into singing the chorus.

"I have a mouth full of food," I protest, but Mom loves music. Other than baking, it's her only passion in life. So, when she chair-dances or belts out a few notes —terribly out of tune, but very earnest—you join in.

What I don't expect is the smile that covers Eagle's entire face as I sing. I flush, finish the chorus to "We Are Family," then jam my mouth full of potato salad. "No more," I tell them. "You're all embarrassing me."

Danielle whoops and slaps the table, and even Mama looks more at ease than I've seen her in a long time. Ruby is actually lying at Eagle's feet. For someone she just met this morning, she seems to have accepted him. She is offering herself to him fully, without hesitation.

After we eat, Mom and Danielle hustle out the door for the movie, telling me to leave the dishes and relax. They both give Eagle a big hug, Danielle comically measuring the size of Eagle's bicep between her fingers —it takes both hands—and then giving me a very obvious thumbs-up. All of which seems to make Eagle laugh even harder.

"Whole lot of estrogen in this place," he teases after Mom and Danielle are gone.

"Yep. Even my dog's a girl," I say, walking into his open arms.

We stand together in the living room behind the closed door. My hands are locked behind his back, and he's slid his hands behind my neck, tugging lightly with his fingers on the loose strands of my hair.

He breathes in deeply and exhales against the top of my head. "I did bring something else for you," he says, his low tone a rumbling storm cloud. I feel the energy in his chest, the promise of power unleashed, unrestrained.

"Follow me," I say, tugging his hand and dragging him to my room.

Once we're inside, I close the door to keep Ruby from joining us. He's toeing off his motorcycle boots, and I just watch him, taking in everything about him. He's so different from Dylan. Different from every man I've dated, and yet, I should feel afraid. Should be worried that this, like everything else before him, won't last.

All I know is, looking at him, the last thing I can feel is fear. I shouldn't trust my body, and yet my fingers are aching to touch him, to explore every inch, every freckle and wrinkle.

"What is it?" he asks, standing after setting his boots off to the side. "Something wrong?"

He looks so concerned. I want to reassure him, but I don't have the words. I don't know how to say what I'm feeling. It's like no feeling I've had before, and I don't want to trust it.

"I want to see your tattoos," I say in a rush, trying to find something to say that makes more sense than what I'm feeling.

He nods slowly. "Okay. Show-and-tell?"

I smile. "It'll be all you showing and you telling. I don't have any tattoos."

He smirks at that. "I saw a scar or two that I think have stories."

I gasp, not believing he noticed those. But I shouldn't be surprised. I nod. "Okay. You first."

He grabs the hem of his T-shirt and pulls it up to reveal his toned stomach. Then higher, revealing a smattering of hair on his chest and defined pecs. Then he tugs the whole damn thing over his head.

I can't help it. I sigh out loud, and he shakes his head with a grin. "I hope that was a happy sound," he says.

"Definitely happy," I say.

He sits down on the side of the bed, and I climb behind him and kneel on the mattress. I trace my fingers along the curved, sharp muscles of his shoulders.

Finally, I get to see everything, and I'm going to take my time. A bald eagle covers his back, the beak and face right between his shoulder blades, the tips of the eagle's wings resting on each shoulder. The navy-blue ink is faded. It could be twenty years old, but the artwork itself is impressive.

I touch the eagle's wings, running my fingertips along the feathers, the scales on its feet with claws inked to razor-sharp-looking points. "This is gorgeous," I tell him. "Absolutely beautiful."

I move from his shoulders and back to his right arm. His bicep is covered in freckles, no doubt from years in the sun, but I can see the logo of what must be his old club, a different version from the one on the back of his jacket, on his inner bicep.

"The club means a lot to you?" I ask, stroking his skin.

"Hmmm," he grunts, nodding. "I only put shit on my skin that means something big, something real to me."

I bite my lip, curious what the club means to him,

how he became involved in it. This is supposed to be show-and-tell, but I don't feel like talking. Show-and-feel would be a better name for this game because all I want to do is touch him, trace the lines of his body and his ink, and memorize every beautiful detail.

"What's this mean?" I ask. On his right hand, he's got the number 1 tattooed on his thumb, an N for neutral on his index finger, 2, 3, and 4 on his other fingers, and a gorgeous number 5 on the top of his hand.

I kiss each of the fingertips on his right hand after he explains the art that decorates them. Then I move to the left.

On his left hand, he's got letters tattooed, two per finger in very small print, starting with his pinkie and leading to his thumb.

CO LA MB AN US

Then, on the back of his left hand, a dotted road that disappears on the horizon.

"St. Colambanus," he explains. "Patron saint of bikers. I'm not a religious man, but I'll take any help I can get. And these fingers pull double duty."

He holds his left thumb and left index finger together, so the -an and -us are joined to make a word.

"When somebody's being a dick, I don't even have to say the word. Just make a finger gun and point the *anus* at 'em. If you get what I mean."

I look down at his fingers. The font does perfectly spell anus when his fingers are pressed together. I shake my head. I can't imagine a man who's a further cry from Dylan.

I kiss the left fingers and then peer around to see what I missed. He's got art on his left arm and lower back under the eagle, so I come full circle, working my way through the stars on his left arm until I see a small word printed on his lower back. It was almost obscured by his underwear when he was first sitting, but now that he's twisted and turned so much, I can see the small black letters spell out a name.

Since everything on Eagle's body seems to stand for something very, very important to him, I have to ask the question, even if it's sensitive. I touch the word, my fingers dipping right below the waistband of his briefs.

"Eagle," I ask, "who's Linda?"

CHAPTER 14
EAGLE

I ANSWER HER QUESTION HONESTLY, "She's someone who used to matter. But she doesn't anymore."

Lacey is behind me, her fingers on the waistband of my boxers, so I can't see her reaction to my explanation. But I feel her lips on my back, and this game of show-and-tell becomes something else altogether.

She breathes hot kisses from the back of my neck to the middle of my spine, sending sparks flaring up and down my arms until my dick is throbbing in my pants.

I turn and face her. "Your turn." I point to the bed, and she lies flat on her back, her head on the pillows.

When she lies down, the cropped T-shirt rides up a bit, exposing her belly. I lie beside her on my side, touching the tiny white scars I spotted on her stomach last night.

"This one?" I ask. I tap a finger along a tiny mark, the well-healed slash not much bigger than a staple.

"They're a set," she explains, waving her hand over

her stomach. "I had my appendix out as a teenager. Laparoscopic surgery scars."

I don't repeat the big word but lower my face to her belly. I kiss my way along each of the scars, the tiny hairs on her stomach standing at attention and goose bumps lifting on her arms. "Mmmm," I hum against her skin, but I am not done. I kiss and breathe hot air, then blow cool against her skin until she shudders.

"Eagle," she whispers.

"You have more," I remind her, then I tug the hem of her T-shirt up farther. She's wearing a soft pink bra, no wires or padding or anything, so there's almost no resistance from the flimsy fabric when I shove the cup aside and expose her right breast.

"Eagle." Her moan is like gasoline tossed on a fire. My dick hardens, and a pulse of needy energy surges through my belly.

I pinch the hard peak between two fingers and gently twist, Lacey squirming against the sheets.

"Oh," she sighs, her eyes closed and her lips slightly parted. "Oh God."

"What's this, then?" I ask, gently touching a square-looking scar along her right nipple.

"I, uh," she pants, dragging in shuddering breaths as I twist and tweak her nipple. "A biopsy and it was benign."

I lower my mouth to the scar and trace the small white tissue, thin and pliable, with the tip of my tongue. "All good now?" I ask.

"God, yes, I'm all good," she says.

"I meant this," I say, cupping her whole breast in my

hand and giving it a gentle squeeze. I suck the nipple into my mouth and stroke my tongue along the delicate skin.

"God, yes," she cries out. "Yes, they're good."

"Yes, they are." And it's never been more true. Her body is soft and curvy, but her tits are full and firm. The kind a man could shove his face into and get lost in forever. I've lusted after this body for too long not to take my time appreciating it now.

I settle myself over her hips and unbutton her denim shorts. She's wearing basic black underwear, and I strip those and the shorts away. I help her pull the T-shirt and bra over her head.

Then she lies back, completely naked. Her light blond hair spills over the pillow, and her brown eyes are open, staring right into mine. I don't break our gaze as I lift her knees and open her legs wide.

"Hold your knees," I whisper, and she does. "Open wide for me," I demand, and she does, a throaty purr bubbling past her lips.

She closes her eyes, and I stick a finger into my mouth to wet it. Then I move through the light curls and find her pussy. I take my time, exploring her lips, moving my finger around and over her flesh, stroking toward her opening to smear her juices onto my finger.

Then, I take my wet fingers and slide up and down her opening, one finger on either side of her clit. She gasps and sighs, wiggling her hips to help me find the right place, the right pressure.

I lower my mouth to her nipple and suck it in,

reaching between us to feel her grow wetter and wetter as I suckle her.

"Eagle," she sighs, rolling her hips lightly and arching her back. "I need more."

But I'm not ready to fuck yet. I lower my mouth to hers and kiss her mouth, tasting the soda she drank at dinner mingling with her unique, sweet flavor. I nudge her opening with one finger while I kiss her, sliding just the tip in, and then go back to her clit, alternating a teasing touch from her lips then back to her clit.

Her breaths are coming in ragged gasps against my mouth, her chest rising and falling as I probe her mouth with my tongue and work her pussy with my fingers. She begins to moan, a consistent, low sound, and starts fucking my hand, working her hips to get me to go inside, deeper.

"How many times can I get you to come for me, baby?" I ask, lifting my face from her skin.

"Are we still playing show-and-tell?" she asks. "Because I'd rather show you than tell you."

"I can get behind that," I say, unzipping my jeans. I only put three condoms back into my wallet, replacing the ones that we used—and the one we wasted. I roll one on before Lacey can even miss my mouth and fingers. Then I settle myself between her legs.

"Hold your knees," I tell her. I want to watch myself fucking her. Want to see what every thrust and tap does to her.

She whimpers but obeys.

"Wider," I tell her. "I want to see you."

Her whole body seems to shudder at my words, and

her mouth parts. She licks her lips and nods, holding her knees wide open. I'm kneeling on the bed, watching her pussy as I anchor myself on her knees and tap the head of my cock against her entrance.

"Mmmm," she cries out, an aching, needy sound. "Eagle…"

"Shh," I remind her. "We're playing show-and-tell. Show me…"

She clenches her pussy.

"Greedy," I tell her, stroking the head of my cock over her drenched slit. "Impatient."

She gasps and nods, her fingers clutching the skin of her knees until the tan under her fingertips turns white. "I want you so bad, Eagle. So bad."

"Show," I urge, and she does, lifting her hips to try to meet my cock. "Uh-huh," I say. "Touch yourself. Touch yourself while I'm inside you."

She releases one knee but keeps both high in the air, her legs spread wide. Then I slide the tip of my cock partway into her pussy. She immediately finds her clit and strokes it in long, rhythmic circles. I work my dick hard, inching in and out of her, edging the shit out of her and bringing myself to a nearly snow-blind state of arousal.

When I finally slide all the way in, Lacey's harsh intake of breath is punctuated by a strangled-sounding scream. She works her clit with her fingers and bucks her hips hard against me. She's bouncing on the bed, and I wish like hell I could see her ass cheeks tighten beneath her. That'll be for round two.

She drops both legs open, whimpers like a wounded

animal, and then opens her mouth to cry out my name. "Fuck, Eagle."

Her hand falls away from her pussy, and all I can feel are her walls clamping down on me. The pressure and the friction are going to be too much, and I wanna fuck her hard before I blow. So, as she's coming, I rest my hands on her knees and thrust hard, deep, sliding through the heat and wet with such power, her tits bounce wildly with every movement. Up and back, in and out, I'm fucking her fast and furious. She's writhing and screaming, clawing at her knees to hold herself wide for me.

Finally, I can't hold back, and I blow, spilling so forcefully into the condom, I can't believe I haven't blown right through the tip.

My heart is pounding, and Lacey is flushed and sweating when I finally collapse on top of her. "Too heavy?" I ask.

"Show, not tell," she mumbles, shaking her head and wrapping her arms around me. She holds me tightly to her, and I relax, trusting that she'll shove me off and show me I'm hurting her before I actually do.

I close my eyes and let my heart thud wildly against her chest. I can feel her breasts squished beneath me. Can feel the heat of her body, the relaxed muscles, and the touch of her hands that seem to pull me closer.

I may not deserve this woman, but I'm here. And I'm going to make the most of every second. I know all too well how quickly a good thing can be gone.

CHAPTER 15
LACEY

I AM SO NOT ready for Monday morning. I wake up at the crack of dawn, and every muscle in my body reminds me of what I did this weekend. I'm exhausted and feel so, so good lying here, I keep my eyes closed and just savor how sore every muscle in my legs and ass are.

I don't think I've ever worked so hard having sex before, but I love it. Holding my legs open, thrusting back against Eagle while lying on my back.

Phew.

No wonder some of the hottest celebrities say their only form of exercise is having sex. I've clearly been doing it wrong my entire adult life.

Besides, I would ordinarily have the Monday after a weekend-long event off. A chance to sleep in and rest, then I'd debrief with the team on Tuesday. But not today. Don told me when he sent me home Saturday to come in this morning so we could meet as a team and discuss what happened this weekend.

I groan as I drag myself from the bed and let Ruby out into the yard. Mom is sleeping in today, and I shush Ruby as I let her out the sun-room door and then back inside for her breakfast. I'll walk her before I leave, but first, I need coffee.

After I feed Ruby and suck down a nice cup of coffee, I take a shower and dry my hair in my bedroom, so it's quiet for Mom. Then, the nerves start to creep in.

I try to remember everything Mom said, everything I believe. I did nothing wrong. I had a relationship with a man who I did not know was married. I didn't know he was a client of the Lantana until shortly before the wedding.

I did nothing wrong.

He's the one who was married.

Is married.

After walking Ruby around the block so she can sniff the local smells and do her business, I put on a power outfit, my standard pencil skirt and blouse. I pull out a reliable pair of pointy-toe flats today. I don't know why. The athletic sex I had with Eagle has my legs feeling wobbly. Maybe that's a good thing. Maybe it's my nerves for what I'm about to face.

I kiss Ruby goodbye and leave a note for Mom, telling her to have a nice day. It's a small thing we do for each other every now and then. Yeah, I could text her, but she's asleep. And when she wakes up, seeing a real smiley face that I drew and not an emotion dumped into a message really will give my mother a huge smile.

I blast the AC vents and head toward work, willing

the butterflies in my stomach to settle down. About half a mile from work, I have to pull over. It's like I'm overcome with this sense of dread, as if something bad's about to happen.

It was the same kind of feeling I got with Dylan at least a half dozen times. Like when he'd answer a phone call a little too fast or when he locked his phone screen as I got close. It was never one big thing that snagged my attention, but tiny moments that cut me like a thousand little paper cuts until, finally, I felt the pain. And then, of course, I bled.

Each time, I ignored all the little signs, and did I ever learn to regret it.

I put on my turn signal and pull into a gas station, off to the side where no one is pumping gas. I blast the AC toward my chest, trying to calm myself and cool down the sweat that's broken out on my lip. "What is wrong with me?"

I look in the rearview mirror as I literally have to pull tissues out of my purse to blot the sweat. I feel weak and nervous, scared and anxious.

Stop this, I tell myself. *You're okay. You did nothing wrong. You might be a little embarrassed, but that's it. You'll get through this. You've gotten through so much worse.*

I check my watch and cringe. I'm in danger of being late if I sit here for any longer, but I turn off the car, run inside the gas station, and buy a bottle of water. It's not really cold, but I pay and rush back to my car, thankful for anything to cut through the dryness of my mouth.

I grab my phone, open my messages, and send off two words to Eagle.

Me: Kinda panicking

I add the worried-face emoji and hit send.

He replies in under thirty seconds. It's like he had his phone in his hands.

Eagle: Where do I need to be? Are you safe?

I smile, relieved that all I'd have to do is ask and he'd drop everything and show up.

Me: I'm okay. On my way to work. It's all just hitting me. Thanks for being there.

Eagle: You want me to come to the Lantana? No charge for security services as long as I'm protecting YOU.

I read his message like three times, not believing what I'm seeing. I know I have to stop comparing every man I date to all the shitty ones who came before him, but...Eagle is special.

But Eagle isn't my boyfriend. I mean, we're adults, and until we have more time or have a talk or something, we're in this vague, undefined space. We've had sex, but we haven't ever seen each other outside of work, except, of course, for the places we've had sex. And yet I texted him early on a Monday morning, and he was there. Ready to jump in and help.

Me: Just hearing from you helps. Thx.

I add the kissy-lips emoji and hit send. Then I put on my big-girl panties and head into work. I got this. No matter what lies ahead. I got this.

———

What I got when I arrived at work was fired.

"Excuse me?" I look from Don to Sergio Lantana to Carla, my head a boiling stew of their words that come together and yet still make no sense. "They said what?"

Sergio Lantana looks down at his extremely tanned hands. "Lacey, you've been a part of this organization so long, I don't know what we'd do without you. But the Acostas have made some serious allegations."

"Allegations," I cry, "what allegations?"

After Sergio sat me down with Carla and Don and said they had no choice but to let me go, all the rest got lost. But before I get up and clear out my office, I need the details. I need to know exactly why I'm being let go.

Sergio, a lovely man who has played Santa at the Lantana employee holiday party every year since I was hired, looks like he's feeling sick. Can't be worse than I feel, though, so I force myself to meet his eyes as he avoids mine.

"Look, Lacey, I don't want to know about any personal relationship you may or may not have had with Dylan Acosta. He's said there was something, and that's not even what matters here. The bride is claiming that you used your influence over her father to steer them into choices that were different from what she stated they wanted for their event."

"What?" I can't even believe my ears. I slam my palms against the conference room table. I can't believe that Carla and Don are here for this. I'm embarrassed, yes, but I'm not even being given a chance to defend myself. "Can you please just—"

Don pulls a file folder out from a stack of papers

he's brought with him. He opens the folder—one that I notice has my last name and the date printed on a label, and I feel the bile rise in my throat—and then he hands me a copy of a contract.

"Lacey, the Acosta bride says that she didn't want the buffet-style brunch at Lantana. She originally said that she wanted a plated brunch at a separate venue. But you—her words, not mine—oversold them on the idea that they should book all three days here. They claim you knew they wanted plated brunch service and that the bride specifically said she didn't want any family-style or buffet-style service." Don sighs and uses air quotes as he says, "The Acostas think anything other than plated service is tacky.'"

Sergio points to the contract. "Dylan Acosta claims that you entered into a relationship with him and used your influence on him to convince him that our venue would be the best value and the best experience for his daughter."

"That's bullshit!" I cry out, shocked. "Look," I tell him, holding out my hand for Don's copy of the contract. "Look at the dates."

Don hands me the contract so I can see for myself, and I'm shocked. Horrified, in fact. The date that Dylan Acosta signed the contract for the wedding itself was a year before we started seeing each other. But he did sign the contract for the full three-day weekend event—rehearsal dinner and brunch the day after the wedding—exactly two weeks *after* we first hooked up.

"I-I guess I misremembered," I stammer, pointing to the date. "By the time they decided to have the three-day event here, I..." I can't say it. I know damn well that I didn't coerce the Acostas into anything. They wanted the three-day package. They asked for it. I even remember Dylan joking after he signed the contract for the full event that he hoped I worked on commission. I joked back that I did not.

I didn't think at the time that it was odd that he came in alone to sign the contract. By then, we'd already slept together, and I had no memory of the fact that he was a father of a bride whom I'd met once for about two hours a year earlier when they toured the facility and then put down a deposit.

It was only later, after we started seeing each other, that he found out I worked at the Lantana and came in to purchase a full package for his daughter. But he said at the time there was no one else he'd trust his daughter's big day to.

Trust. His word, not mine.

And now, all that trust is shattered. And he's accusing me of inappropriate behavior. All the black-and-white print of the employee handbook swims before my eyes. Isn't this exactly the kind of thing the handbook was written to prevent?

I have to admit, it looks bad any way you slice it.

I look up at Sergio. "I made a bad choice in my personal life," I say, holding my chin high. "But I did nothing to compromise the integrity of my position or the Lantana itself. I can assure you, Sergio, I handled the Acostas like every other client. With integrity and with their best interests at heart."

My words fall heavy on the room. I look at Carla,

but she's always been my assistant. Never a full wedding planner. Three years ago, when we signed the Acostas, she was still learning the customer relations software we use to manage our contacts. I can't expect her to remember the facts if even I didn't. I can't expect her to defend me, to step in and speak up, when she didn't know the ins and outs of the situation.

What I do know with all my heart and soul is that I did nothing wrong.

"Please understand," I say quietly. "Dylan Acosta wanted the three-day event. The bride herself signed and initialed the final menu, as well as the final head count just before the ceremony. What could they possibly hope to accomplish by saying I coerced them?"

Sergio sighs and shrugs. "Lacey, they are wealthy people. You gave them a black eye with the people at the club by embarrassing Olivia at her daughter's wedding." I try to interrupt that no one even knew anything happened, and there was no way I embarrassed her, but he waves a hand in the air. "Buffets are tacky, and the bride says you boxed her into a corner and said there was no time to make any changes. You apparently said that they were getting a buffet because that's what the contract said they could have."

"They are twisting my words." The truth comes out of me, but it feels like barbed wire getting pulled through my stomach. "I did say that, but later. After the final contracts were signed. Not to coerce them. What good would it do me to undersell them? Plated breakfasts cost twice what the buffet option costs. It just doesn't make any sense why I would sell them something cheaper than the most expensive services."

"Lacey," Sergio says softly. "They're suggesting that because you tried to strike up a relationship with Dylan and he shot you down, that you were in a position to manipulate the event and make them look bad, give them an experience far inferior to what they'd expect from the Lantana."

I'm speechless at that. The argument has Dylan written all over it, and I just can't fight that kind of warped logic. Everyone in this room knows that if the bride had given us even three days' notice, we would have moved heaven and earth to give them a plated brunch.

Look at what we did with the tuxedos. I hired a tailor, dragged two bikers in on their days off, and convinced them, with just a couple days' notice, to do something we normally never do. That's customer service. That's what I do. I deliver prestige experiences to my customers. I deliver on the fantasy.

Angry tears burn my eyes, but I won't cry. "So, you have to take their side because they will complain to their friends," I say quietly. "And business for the Lantana plummets all because Dylan Acosta twists the truth into something it's not."

Sergio looks down at his hands, while Don quietly slides the contract back into its folder.

Only Carla speaks up. "It's not too late to quit, maybe," she says softly. "That way, you wouldn't have to have a termination on your employment record. That would help with unemployment, job references."

Sergio shoots her a sharp look, but I'm immediately ready to drop to her feet and hug her. Instead, I nod to my boss of eight years.

"Sergio, I'd prefer not to have to hire an attorney to look over the contract I have. There is nothing in the contract that says I can't sell a customer one product over another."

"Lacey, you slept with one of our clients." Sergio slaps his forehead loudly. "What do you expect me to do here?"

"Fine," I say, standing up. I halfway wish I were wearing heels. I tower over Sergio even in flats, but I wish I could be stronger, bigger, taller than these small people who want to bring me down. It has to be enough that they can't. That I won't let them.

"Will you allow me to go to my office and write out a formal letter of resignation?" I ask, my eyes never leaving Sergio's face. "Will you accept that as a compromise instead of firing me?"

Sergio takes a long, deep breath, the gold ring on his pinkie finger glittering in the reflection of the gilt-frame mirrors that line the conference room. "Fine," he says. "But Lacey, there's one more thing."

I grab my purse and stand. "What?"

"Olivia Acosta says you threw the tablet on the ground at them, at her, and that's why it broke. I'm going to have to dock your final paycheck for reckless treatment of company property."

I stand up and cross my arms. "You're seriously kidding me?" I ask. "She said that? You know there was a witness? The security..." I let the words die on my lips. I do not want to drag Eagle into this—not in any way, shape, or form. "Did you check the security footage? Did you try to verify that what she said was how it happened? Did it ever occur to you that she could have grabbed the tablet and thrown it at me?"

"Did she?" Sergio challenges, sounding angry now. "Because I don't see a workplace safety incident report. And as you're the director of events, if that did happen, it would have been on you to complete that form, to put a hold on the security footage, and to immediately obtain witness names and contact information so we could investigate that event. Is that what you're trying to say happened, Lacey?"

The owner of the place I have loved for so, so long is now looking at me with contempt. He was annoyed, maybe frustrated earlier. My behavior put him in a bad spot, and I get that. But this? Now, he's basically accusing me of lying.

"I'm not saying that's what happened," I tell him. "But the Acostas had ample opportunity to report any inappropriate behavior or violence."

"And they did," Don says, looking grim. "As soon as their daughter's brunch was over. They said they were afraid of retaliation."

"But I wasn't even at the damn brunch. How could I retaliate?" I want to scream, throw something. How could one bad decision—okay, I dated Dylan for fourteen months, so hundreds, probably thousands of bad decisions—spiral to this point? I hardly know what's happening, which end is up. All I know is in the space of a single weekend, everything I love has been taken from me.

My job.

My dignity.

My professionalism.

My reputation.

Instead of fighting with Sergio and Don, I gather my things quietly. I take a soft breath and look over the beautiful room, the pink marble and rich wallpaper now cloying in its ostentatious colors.

"Given that we aren't seeing the situation from the same perspective, I feel as though I'll need to get a lawyer to protect me, my reputation, and my future employment prospects. I'd appreciate if you'd wait to take any final action until you hear from that person."

Don nods. "You have five days left of accrued vacation," he says.

It weighs heavy on my heart that he came prepared with that information. Even I don't know how much vacation time I have accrued. I hardly ever use it.

Don continues, "You can use that time to sort out your next step. If we don't hear from your lawyer by Monday, we'll issue a formal letter explaining what we've decided."

I look over the faces of these people I've loved, worked with, laughed with for years. "May I clear out my office of my personal effects?" I ask, tears threatening to spill from my burning lids.

"They had me take care of that yesterday." Carla sounds so apologetic. She slides a plain brown banker's box from under the conference room table. "This was everything I could find, Lacey. But if you think of anything I missed…"

I swipe a single tear from my cheek then silently take the box. "Thank you, Carla," I say. It's not her fault. None of this is anyone's fault except my own. No matter how pure my intentions may have been, every road I took over the last two years has led me to this moment.

I made this bed. And now it's time to lie down in it.

I turn and walk slowly through the building, acceptance and guilt flaming my cheeks beet red. I can feel the heat radiating off them as I pass Bob at the front desk. I want to say goodbye, to wish the sweet man all my best, but feeling the heavy eyes of Sergio Lantana, Don, and Carla following us, Bob firms his lips and turns his back to me. He's an old man who needs his job just as much as I needed mine.

I swallow hard, then exit for what will probably be the last time through the glass doors. I don't let myself look back. I walk to the employee lot just like I did Saturday—dejected and confused. Only this time, I have no hope of going back to my dream job.

Leave it to one shitty man and a truckload of stupidity to ruin a girl's dreams.

CHAPTER 16
EAGLE

WHEN I RIDE up to Lacey's place, she's standing on the front porch, dressed in jeans, running shoes, a long-sleeved shirt, and sunglasses. Her hair is swept up in a bun, and the rattling in my heart when I see her matches the rumble of the bike—steady and strong and so loud, I'm sure everybody can hear it.

I don't know what this means. I don't catch feelings. I'm not a guy who puts his heart out there. In fact, since Linda, I've kept it buried in the deepest, darkest parts of me. It's better that way. Sex and love don't have to go ahead in hand, and it's much fucking easier when they don't.

She rushes down the concrete path to greet me. I climb off the bike, meet her on the sidewalk, and pull her into my arms.

Neither one of us says anything. When she called me after she got canned from the Lantana, she was so upset, crying so hard, she couldn't tell me what happened. It didn't take a rocket scientist to guess. Shit rolls downhill, pure and simple. I told her to wear something that covers her arms and legs. That I was taking her someplace.

She wraps her arms around me tight, then pushes the sunglasses off her face to peer at me. "You don't wear a helmet?" she asks worriedly. "Eagle…"

"Brought one for you," I tell her.

She looks like she wants to argue, but she just nods. We head over to the bike.

"This your first time?" I ask.

She bites her lower lip, looking worried. "Mmm-hmm."

I turn to her and hold her chin in my hand. "Hey, hey, don't be scared. I've been riding these things since I was knee-high to a grasshopper. You hold on to me tight and just keep your body relaxed. Follow my lead. You feel me lean; you lean with me. Don't try to pull me back."

"Sounds like dancing," she smiles. But then her face falls. "I'm a terrible dancer. You should know that."

I grin. "But you're a rock star in bed, and riding this is a lot more like riding me than dancing."

Her mouth falls open, but then she shakes her head. "Okay. I trust you."

I get her situated on the bike, make sure she knows where to rest her feet, and then adjust the helmet on her head.

"Oh wow," she says. "I can see why you don't wear this. It's hard to see."

"You wear yours," I tell her. "And you just look straight ahead, over my shoulder, if you can. It's your first time, so just get used to the noise of the bike and the feel of the road."

She gets off the bike, I get on, and then she slides in tight behind me. I call over my shoulder to her. "I won't be able to hear you, so unless something's wrong, we'll talk when we get there."

She nods, and I feel her hands tighten around my waist like she's holding on for dear life. I grab her hands with mine and squeeze, then fire up the engine.

It's loud, but it's like the opening notes of my favorite song coming on the radio. When I first hear that roar, something blazes through my body.

It's the same feeling I used to get when the MC was dirty. My old man always thought there was a little darkness in me—a hunger for violence, for chaos, that most of the time I kept suppressed. Maybe I learned that the only easy way for guys like me sometimes does require going off the beaten path, forging our own way.

Or maybe, I just love the ride.

I pull away from the curb and hear a little happy squeal in Lacey's chest. I grin, the glare of the sun reflecting off my shades, as I steer us toward one of my favorite rides.

I can feel her body relax the longer we ride. At stoplights, she turns her head ever so slightly and looks around. I hope she loves it. Hope she loves it even half as much as I do.

I take the backroads to a small state park about fifteen minutes away from Lacey's. We ride through the long, winding one-lane road that leads to a parking lot.

"Bus stops here," I say, parking and climbing off. I

help Lacey out of the helmet and search her face. "You okay? Like it so far, or are you scared shitless?"

Her face is elated as she shakes her head. "That. Was. Incredible." She looks back at the bike reverently. "I had no idea. I've never experienced anything like that. I mean, I get it. I totally get it."

I nod and motion for her to follow me, but deep down, my heart's bursting open. Women usually love the bike, especially after their first time. But Lacey's got a way of expressing herself that makes me feel proud. Like I'm the only one who could have shown her this kind of good time. Maybe she would feel this way with any asshole who took her for a ride, but the way she looked from me to the bike, like she wanted to caress us both and couldn't pick where to start... It feels good. Lacey makes me feel good. Better about myself than literally anything ever has.

Feeling a little more confident, I take her hand, and together, we walk over a small wooden bridge. Lacey walks slowly, peering over the bridge and into the water.

"Whatcha looking for?" I ask.

She smiles. "Whatever there is to see. Lily pads, algae. I just like to know what lives here."

I nod and slow my steps so she can look. I've got to admit, I don't stop and smell the roses all that often. I stare through the dark shades, but I can't see too much that's all that interesting. And then, I see movement.

"There," I point.

"I see it." Lacey's voice is a hushed whisper.

It's just a lizard, nothing we don't see a thousand of

scattering through parking lots and across lawns all over the place. But somehow, seeing that here, where the bugger can live free of the dangers of the human world, hits different. I've been here a hundred times, but I've never noticed a lizard. I tighten my grip on Lacey's hand and wonder what else I'll experience with her that feels new.

We walk slowly, the crunch of our footsteps on the path the only sound. It's Monday, so other than a few people hiking, this place will be pretty deserted.

That's why I picked it.

After about a five-minute walk, the path curves, and I can see what we came here for. Lacey spots it before I can even point it out.

"Oh my God," she says, pointing. "That is beautiful. In a haunting kind of way, but it's gorgeous."

I nod, letting her take it in. I wonder if she knows what it is, what it's called. I don't know much about the natural world. Open the hood of a car or show me a disassembled bike engine, and I can tell you what every piece does and where it belongs, when the machine is sick or old or just needs a little TLC to get back to its original glory.

I lead Lacey to the massive tree that doesn't look like one tree at all. There are clearly a trunk and branches under there, but growing up, around, and through the tree are vines and leaves, branches from other trees.

I tell her what little I know. "I used to call this the witch trees," I say with a laugh. "I was scared of them. My mom would take me on long walks when my old man would be in a mood. For a long time, I thought these trees were mean old witches who came out when my dad got mad."

Lacey tightens her fingers around mine as she listens. "But my mama told me, no, they're survivors. Some people see them as pests—trees that kill other trees and basically eat 'em up and grow right in, around, and through the space left by the original tree."

I stop and think of my mama, God rest her soul.

"My mother always taught me to be the survivor," I explain. "Find a way through. And don't let anybody tell you you're ugly." I chuckle and point at my face. "I didn't always look like this."

"Gorgeous?" Lacey fills in, smiling with one corner of her mouth. "I don't believe it."

She squeezes my fingers again.

"I think it's beautiful," she says. "I can see why you'd think they are witchy trees, though," she says, releasing my hand to walk forward and lightly run her fingertips over the bark.

Some of the leaves that climb the tree are vibrant green, and some are brown. Lacey tenderly strokes a green leaf. "Life right there alongside death. Beautiful. Complicated."

I nod, and we sit on the packed dry dirt under the tree. The canopy of all the other trees in the park provides plenty of shade, so even in our jeans and long-sleeved shirts, it's cool.

Lacey leans against me, and I throw an arm over her shoulder.

"I did it, you know," she says softly. "I did have a relationship with Dylan Acosta."

I hold up a hand to stop her. "Don't need to know," I tell her. And I'm honestly not sure I want to hear about it. The thought of her with that asshole... His entitled, slick face, his shitty grin. I hate men like that. Used to take great pride in not being a man like that. I don't know how Lacey can want to be with someone like him and also with someone like me.

It's like she's reading my mind, though, because she explains it. "I never cared about him in the way I wanted to. You know..." She laughs, but it's a dry, bitter sound. "I always wanted the fairy tale. I always wanted love to solve everything. To come with laughter and happiness, total acceptance and fun."

She shakes her head. "Dylan lied to me," she says. "About so many things. But the worst part is that I lied to myself."

I can only imagine the bullshit that man fed a woman like Lacey. Anything to get into her pants, because of course, he took one look at her and wanted her. Who wouldn't.

"I lied to myself about who he was, what we had. I believed the stupidest things, Eagle, and you know why?" She's not crying, but she rubs at her eyes. "Because I wanted something so bad that I refused to believe what I had right in front of me wasn't it. Could never be it." She turns to face me. "Did you ever want something so badly that you made yourself believe something that wasn't real? Maybe wasn't even true?"

At first, I think no. But then I wonder. Maybe I have. The Disciples hasn't been the club I joined for a long time now. I'm not the man I was when I joined, but that doesn't mean I don't keep looking for the same thrills—the easy money, the bonds that were tighter than blood, the excitement.

When we were dirty, I was happy. Now that we're a bunch of washed-up construction workers and security guards, yeah, I am still tight with my brothers. But things have changed.

Problem is, I haven't.

And I still keep looking for what we used to be.

I look at Lacey and can understand exactly what she means. Even with Linda, I was telling myself stories that were probably never true. That I had to be the stand-up guy. That I had to do this, take that.

"Yeah," I finally tell her. "I have. I get it."

She turns to me and lifts her face, then kisses me on the lips lightly. "I really like you, Eagle," she says quietly. "I don't want what I feel with you to be a story I'm telling myself."

Her words hit hard as I realize that I feel the same way. That vague sense of discomfort, the uneasy feeling that I've been braced for. We've known each other for two years, but this is different. We've never known each other like this. Our bodies connected; our minds honest. Maybe even our hearts involved in some way…

"This," I tell her, "feels real to me. I don't think anything's ever felt this real."

I hold her face in my hands and kiss her, sweeping my tongue across her lips until she opens for me. A soft moan whispers against my mouth as our tongues clash. We kiss like that for a few long minutes, neither one of us wanting the kiss to end. But there's more to it.

There's feeling behind these kisses. A grasping and a desperation for more. We don't just want to keep kissing. Neither one of us wants the honesty to end. The truth that we've shared is something. Means something.

She pulls her face gently from mine and sighs. "I'm unemployed," she says, "and I need to find an attorney. I have until Friday to negotiate a mutually agreeable separation from the Lantana."

The blood boils through my entire body at that. "The fuckers," I say. I don't know much about lawyers —I've spent my whole life trying to avoid the law at all costs. But I do know one. "I might be able to help," I tell her.

She looks at me curiously. I pull out my phone and tap out a few texts, and I notice I have yet another one from Linda. But I refuse to let that bitch ruin my morning.

I silence my phone and stand.

"Come on," I tell Lacey. "Let's see if we can make these fuckers pay."

CHAPTER 17
LACEY

THE MOTORCYCLE CLUB actually has an attorney. And while that alone surprised me, what got me even more shocked was the man's name.

Eagle nods at the man behind the desk. He looks old, and he could definitely use some modern technology. His desk is covered with papers, some so yellow, they can't be part of active cases. He's smoking cigarettes, and when he's not smoking, a thin line of smoke drifts from the cigarette in the ashtray by his phone toward the ceiling.

"Lacey Mercer, Lacey Mercer." The man cocks his head as though he's thinking about whether he knows me, but then he sticks out a tobacco-stained hand. "Call me Fingers."

Fingers, which is yet another club nickname, is a real lawyer, if you believe the single framed degree on the wall, but I'm not exactly filled with confidence at first sight.

I look from him to Eagle, not sure where or how to begin.

Eagle nods, quietly telling me to trust Fingers with my most private shame. "You want me to leave?" Eagle asks.

I shake my head. He's going to learn the whole truth eventually. It might as well come out now, before I get in too deep. Before I start to really fall.

"Well, Mr. Fingers," I start.

"Just Fingers." He takes a long draw on his cigarette and blows the smoke respectfully in the opposite direction of where I'm sitting. "Go on," he urges.

He's not taking any notes but leans back in his chair and listens as I explain. "Well, I had a brief relationship with a man who I thought was single, a widower, actually. That was a lie, as I found out later. Turns out, the man is the father of a bride who booked her wedding at the venue where I work—or worked."

"Where's that? What venue?" Fingers asks.

"Villa Lantana." I don't expect him to have heard of it because Fingers doesn't exactly look like the kind of guy who attends many weddings or upscale events, but he nods.

"Sergio Lantana. Nice guy, for the most part." Fingers taps the side of his head. "Give me a second." He closes his eyes and seems to be thinking. "I'll have to have my girl run a conflicts check," he says, although I saw no girl and don't know what a conflicts check is.

My face must give that away, so he explains.

"I gotta decent memory despite all the drugs I did in the seventies," he cough-laughs, and Eagle smirks.

"Guess I did the right kinds of drugs. Anyway." He taps his head again. "I don't think I've ever represented Lantana in the past, but I'll have my part-time girl check. If I ever did any work for the guy, I couldn't help in a case against him now. But I think we're clear. Go on."

I explain in the very barest detail how Olivia must have found out about the affair at the rehearsal or after it. I tell him about the wedding, how Don sent me home, and the allegations that the Acostas later made against me.

Fingers blows air through his mouth, and I think I feel the tiniest bit of spittle hit my face, but I don't dare lift my hand to wipe it away. "Employment cases. Handled a million of 'em."

He asks me a bunch of personal questions, like how long I worked for the Lantana, how much I made. If I worked on commission or if I was ever pressed to upsell clients on any product or service. I answer honestly. No, no, it's a salaried job that I always loved. We never had to use heavy-handed tactics to sell things. We charged a lot of money because we were the best, and our clients expected to pay for that.

"Sergio got any other disgruntled former employees? Or current employees, for that matter?" Fingers asks.

I shake my head. "We have no turnover. My assistant is the most recent new hire, and she's been there over three years. People love the place. We get hired and don't leave." I frown because that reputation is definitely going to stop me from finding another job.

There's no moving up from the Lantana. Only moving on.

Fingers seems to get this as he charges on with a plan. "I need to see everything," he tells me. "Anything you ever signed and anything they made you sign, even if you don't have copies of it. You got the employee handbook? Your evaluations?"

We talk through what I have, and he makes a list, writing things down for the first time. Then, as if it only just occurs to him, he looks at me and points a pencil in my direction. "What do you want?" he asks me. "In these situations, we usually go for money or your job back."

I shake my head. "I don't see how I can get my job back. And I don't think I'm entitled to—"

"Ahh-ahh. Never say what you think you're entitled to. That's what the law is for. It'll tell us what's yours and what's not." He writes down a dollar sign and then holds up a hand. "One last question. You got money?"

I look to Eagle, not sure what he means. "I mean, some. I'm not rich, if that's what you mean."

"For me," he explains. "Case like this, I'd normally take on an hourly basis." He explains that, because I don't make a ton of money, the amount he might be able to get me in settlement from the Lantana isn't a lot. If he takes fifteen percent, that brings the amount down even more.

"How'd you get involved in this?" Fingers asks all of a sudden, looking at Eagle.

"Working security at the place," Eagle says. "I got up close and personal with Acosta when he grabbed

Lacey's arm at the rehearsal dinner. Been wondering if me putting him in his place has anything to do with him trying to put Lacey in her place on the wedding day. It all feels pretty tit for tat to me."

Fingers slams a hand down on the desk, and a bunch of papers shift around. Miraculously, nothing falls off, but his cigarette does wobble out of his ashtray. Fingers grabs it and bites it between his teeth. "He assaulted her? He touched her? Why the hell didn't you say so sooner?"

I start to interrupt. This could go way too far. "He didn't assault me," I rush to explain. "He grabbed my wrist, but—"

Fingers holds up a cigarette like a finger to silence me. "Don't you worry. We're not going to lie and say you're hurt or traumatized. We deal with the facts, and the fact is, if a guest touched you, laid his hand on you, there could be a bodily injury component to this deal. That means insurance might pay, there could be a claim…"

He looks excited for a minute, but then he explains. "The messier we make this for Sergio, the more he's gonna want this over and done with. If I tell him I have a premises bodily injury claim he needs to report to his insurance company, he's gonna freak out. Most insurance policies don't cover that shit."

I'm literally lost. I have no clue what any of this means. "Are you going to sue Sergio?" I ask. I don't think I can handle that. I don't think I want that, even if it's potentially something I'm entitled to. I don't like any of this. I just want it over. I want my job back. I want the fantasy. But unless Fingers can turn back time, I know I'm in for a painful disappointment.

"No lawsuit yet," Fingers says. "That shit's expensive, and we don't want him to lawyer up. I'm going to shake the tree. Send a letter. See what falls out."

He stands up and shakes my hand over the desk. "No charge for today," he says, nodding at Eagle. "You're with this guy?"

I look to Eagle, who answers for me. For us.

"Will being with me hurt her case?" Eagle asks carefully.

Shit. I never thought about that.

Fingers gives Eagle a crooked smile. "Attorney-client privilege."

Eagle nods. "We're together," he confirms.

Fingers nods. "About time you got yourself an old lady," he says. "I hope this one sticks around."

Eagle doesn't blink, doesn't respond to that. Fingers charges on. "I go way back with Eagle and his brothers," Fingers says, "So, I'll send a letter to Sergio and see what he says. If I can help you, I'll do it on the cheap."

I sign a retention agreement and fee disclosure. It all scares me, but Eagle stands over me and reads the docs. "It's all right," he assures me. "You can trust Fingers. He won't do you wrong."

Since I don't have time to shop for a lawyer, I sign the papers, trusting my fate and my future to a man named Fingers. No, that's not true. Eagle brought me here. I'm trusting my fate and my future to a man called Eagle.

Eagle and Fingers slap each other on the back, talk for a couple minutes about people named Morris and Crow, then names I recognize—Brute and Tiny and some others. After, Eagle grabs my hand, and we leave the small office.

Once we're out in the afternoon sun, I take a long breath of the humid but blissfully smoke-free air.

"You all right?" Eagle asks.

I don't answer right away. I am not okay. I am not okay with communicating with my old company through a lawyer. I'm not okay trusting my fate in the hands of someone who knows my secrets but doesn't know me.

And worse than that, I'm scared. Scared that I'm in too deep with Eagle. I'm trusting him, but not only that, I'm trusting people he trusts. What's to stop Fingers from sending a letter, sending me a bill, and getting nothing done to help me? What's to stop Eagle from blocking my phone, dropping me like a hot rock once I have no job? Will he keep working at the Lantana?

"Lacey?" I feel Eagle's rough but now-familiar hand snake along the back of my neck. He lowers his face to mine and kisses me lightly. "Hey," he says. "It's gonna be okay. Fingers knows his shit. I wouldn't have brought you here if I didn't think you could trust him."

Trust. That word again. It's like the universe is teasing me, tormenting me. Throwing the very thing I do far too easily right in my face. I trusted Dylan. I trusted myself. Am I a fool for trusting Eagle and, through Eagle, this Fingers character?

I grab the helmet and start to put it on, but then I

stop. I need to say something, and I want to say it now. Before we get on the bike and the noise of the engine and the speed of the road distract me from what I'm feeling.

"Eagle," I say, holding the helmet between us like a shield. I look into his face, his sunglasses on the top of his head so I can see into his deep blue eyes. "Please," I whisper, fighting tears. "Don't break my heart. I honestly don't think I could take it."

Eagle's mouth falls open, but then he leans forward and kisses me again. "I won't," he promises, saying the words so firmly I want to believe him. "I won't," he repeats. "You too," he says. "Got it?"

I pull away from his kiss and nod. But I'm not sure what I'm nodding to. Could I ever break his heart? I don't know. But the way I feel right now, one wrong move from this tattooed former employee of mine, and the last of my faith in dreams will shatter. And I don't know if I have the strength to put the pieces together even one more time.

CHAPTER 18
EAGLE

"YO, BROTHER." Crow claps me on the back in greeting.

It's five-freaking-o'-clock in the morning, and I'm standing in the driveway of a modest two-bedroom, one-bath house. Crow's wearing a safety vest and a hard hat, and I have to stifle a laugh. Crow's an ex-con. He did real time for a crime that wasn't intentional, but which cost a man his life anyway. Bar fight gone bad. Crow threw the punch that knocked a guy's lights out for good, and he did serious time for it.

But now, he couldn't look more legit. A wedding band is tattooed where a gold ring would be since in this job, jewelry would be a danger. Like everybody else in the club, Crow's gone domestic. He's got a wife, Birdie, and a stepdaughter, Mia. He's even got a little bit of a belly now, and I smack him on it.

"Married life treating you good?" I ask.

I mean it as a joke, but a cold look crosses over Crow's face. "Yeah, man, all good," he says.

But then, clearly, he's back to business. No time to shoot the shit. He's telling me about the work they're doing on this house, the turnaround time, and it all starts buzzing like static in my ears.

This is the shit I wasn't cut out for. Listening to some jacknob with a hard-on for a paycheck giving me rules and instructions. I try to listen, but I'm out there trying to figure out how Crow became that guy.

At some point, he's like, "You got all that?" And I just nod.

I don't, but what the fuck. It's demolition. How hard could it be? I tear shit out and throw it away.

I follow Crow to a huge pickup truck where he's got a lockbox with extra materials. He gives me a neon vest and a hard hat, and he points down at my boots.

"I'll let those ride today, man, but you gotta wear steel-toe. It's a safety issue. Insurance'll be up my ass." He doesn't even wait for me to answer. He turns and heads through the open door that leads into a really outdated kitchen.

There's no one else here but Crow and me, and he shows me where the sledgehammer, crowbar, and other tools are. He's talking fast and throwing a lot at me, but again, I just drift. This isn't for me. Nothing about this shit is for me.

But what the hell is?

I can't go back to the Lantana. I texted Carla yesterday to let her know that I was giving two-weeks' notice and that I'd find someone to cover my events over those two weeks. I couldn't go back there and work for the asshats who fired Lacey. Brute was fine with it, though. He actually thought Carla was hot, so I'm not exactly putting her in a bind. If Arrow can't cover me, Brute'll find somebody who wants to make a few bucks standing around doing nothing.

Unlike what I'm doing here. There's no AC running and not even a fan since I'll be kicking up dust, tearing out the kitchen cabinets and fixtures, and within an hour, I'm drained and soaked with sweat.

Crow checks in on me, and that's when the shit starts. "Fuck, man." He points at the stack of cabinets I've torn down from the wall. "What the hell did you do?"

I look from him to the cabinets, totally confused. "I did what you told me," I say. "I tore the shit down."

Crow curses under his breath. "Fuck, man," he says. "I told you this row of cabinets here—" he points to a row that's splintered and shattered in a pile on the floor "—we're reusing in the garage. Repurposing." He bends to inspect the damage, but there's no fixing this.

I either didn't hear or didn't pay attention when he said they were gonna try to save one small strip of the cabinets to reuse someplace else.

Crow's muttering about money down the drain, but he just sighs. "There's nothing else to fuck up in here," he says. "Tear it all out."

I am suddenly so pissed off, I want to drive the sledgehammer right through the stack of ruined cabinets. This is why I'm not cut out for honest work. I can't listen. I don't give a shit about repurposing or whatever the hell Crow wants to do here. He shoulda said clear as day, "Don't fuck these up. I need them."

I take my frustration out on the rest of the demolition, knowing full well that Crow probably did tell me not to fuck them up. I need work. I need money. But this ain't me. This isn't how I want to earn it.

My mind goes to a dark place. I miss the old days. The days when we made steady cash and lots of it. There's no easy way for a man like me to make an honest buck. But I made a lot of bucks the not-so-honest way.

I can't, though. The club's clean now. If I wanted to run drugs or move stolen shit, I'd have to betray my brothers. Leave the club, patch in someplace else, but that's something I'd never do. I could freelance and go solo. Find some low-end hacks who need muscle.

The idea fills me with hope, and I wonder why I didn't figure out a way to get back into the shit years ago. But then it hits me. Lacey.

Lacey's the reason I've got a solid employment history, a paycheck, and taxes paid on legit earnings for the last couple of years.

I started at the Lantana when we cut ties with everything that could land us in prison—or, worse, dead at the hands of a rival club. I started at the Lantana because I needed to find my own gig. And I stayed for her.

I don't think I've ever admitted it to myself before. But I see it now. Without Lacey to keep me interested, to keep me coming back, I don't know if I would've stayed straight as long as I have.

As I look over the pile of ruined cabinets, Crow's disappointment written all over his face, I don't know if

I'm going to be able to stay straight now that I don't have the Lantana and her to hold me in place.

By the time lunch rolls around, Crow seems calmer. He's been taking calls all day, lining up contractors and shit. I don't know. But what I do know is I'm ravenous by the time I jump into my truck.

"I'm gonna grab a burrito," I call out to Crow. "You want somethin', man?"

Crow shakes his head. "I got lunch coming up right now."

Just then, a modest red sedan pulls up to the street and parks in front of the house we're working on. The back door opens, and a little girl flings herself from the car and starts running.

Crow opens his arms and scoops her up, giving her a big kiss on the cheek. She's talking a mile a minute, and Crow's completely absorbed in her. So much so that he doesn't seem to notice the beautiful woman who gets out from behind the wheel. But she notices me and waves.

"Eagle." Birdie, Crow's wife, walks up to the passenger window of my truck and leans on the door. "How's it going on your first day?" Birdie's a cool chick. It's obvious that Crow's wrapped around that little kid's finger, but I've always liked his wife.

"Not bad," I lie.

She seems to study my face. "You sure?" she asks, as if she can tell I'm not at all sure about this.

I wave a hand, not seeing any reason to lie. "Not sure all this shit's for me," I say.

Birdie doesn't say anything. She throws a look back

at Crow and then smiles at me. "When Crow first started, he hated it too," she says. "He won't say that now, but he came home every night real quiet." She leans deeper into the window. "It's not easy," she says. "But it gets better."

She gives me a smile and then turns and walks over to Crow. He kisses her and sets Mia on her feet. Then, both of them holding Mia's hands, the three of them head over to Crow's truck.

I wave and fire up my truck, mapping it to a nearby burrito place. Birdie's words stay with me the whole drive. I can only imagine how hard it was for Crow to adjust from being on the inside. He came back to a club that had gone clean, after spending years behind bars with thugs and thieves. To try to find a job with a conviction on his record, to go from the life we all had to a totally new normal. Yeah, I can believe it was hard for him. I can believe it took time.

But as I watch Crow and his family pull away, I wonder if, with the right motivation, I can change. Seems like I did for a while, at least. But what I did it for was not myself. And if I lose Lacey, everything will fall to ash. Just like it did with Linda.

And I can never let that happen to me again.

CHAPTER 19
LACEY

IT'S BEEN a week since Fingers sent a demand letter to Sergio Lantana, and I've been sick with worry every minute. I refresh my emails every ten minutes, more often if I have my phone in my hand.

My mother's been taking all her unused vacation time to stay home with me. I keep telling her not to and that I'm fine, but I think she wants to distract me, make sure I'm not too down.

And I have been down. Lost in my own thoughts. The only moment's break I have from the worry about my job is when I'm with Eagle. He's been working a new construction job all week and hasn't been in the best of moods about it. All I know is when we're together, everything else seems to disappear.

But I can't hide from real life forever, distracting myself with amazing sex with Eagle and binge-watching shows with my mom.

When I finally get an email from Fingers telling me

the Lantana wants to mediate, it felt like the weight of the world lifts off my shoulders.

"Come on," Mom says after I tell her what Fingers set up. "Let's get mani-pedis to celebrate."

I offer to drive since Mom insists on paying, and I try not to worry too much about my bank balance.

The Lantana agreed to keep paying me my regular salary even though I'm not working until we mediate a resolution. I used up all my accrued vacation days, and today is the official first day I'm being paid for a job I'm not doing.

Mom turning up the radio as we drive blasts the worries from my brain. Mom sings along very, very badly with Bruce Springsteen, and I can't help myself. I have to chime in. Even when the world is going to hell, I can still sing with my mama.

The salon is nearly empty when we go in, so we have the massage chairs to ourselves. While our feet soak in piping-hot bubble baths, I rest my head back and close my eyes.

"Do you ever think about your father?" Mom's question shocks me. Not just because she's talking about Dad in public, but because she's talking about him, period.

I whip my head up from the soft cushioned chair, and I look at her. "Yes. I mean, not really. Sometimes. Why?"

My mom shrugs. "Just curious." She leans her head back and closes her eyes.

"Mom, you can't just ask a question like that and

pretend it's no big deal. Why? Did something happen? Did you hear from him?"

She chuckles and opens her eyes. "Nothing that exciting." She lifts her feet from the tub of hot water and wiggles her suds-covered toes. "He got recommended to me the other day," she says quietly. "On social media. He must be a friend of a friend, so the site thought we knew each other." She shrugs, leans her head back, and closes her eyes. "So, I friend-requested him."

My eyes nearly bug out of my head, and I lean forward so far, my feet almost kick over the bowl of water. "Mom, you did what? Did he accept?"

Mom nods. "He did. It took a couple days, but he's not very active on the site. Not like me."

I chuckle at that. My mom doesn't share a lot of personal stuff on social media, but she is the queen of the meme. I've always laughed that memes are an old person's emojis, and Mom lives up to that theory.

"So, tell me," I demand. "Tell me everything."

As I say it, I realize I am genuinely curious. Curious why my mother friend-requested a man who did her so, so dirty. Why she is telling me now.

She smiles. "There's not much to tell. You can check him out, if you want." She holds her phone out to me. "There's not much to see."

I cock my chin at her, curious what she wants me to see. Mom isn't at all secretive about her phone. I know the passcode, and half the time, she asks me to text things to her friends for her because I type so much faster, and she hates correcting typos when she uses voice-to-text.

I reach across the chair for Mom's phone, but I leave it in my lap. I am suddenly filled with the same feeling that I've always had when it comes to my father. I don't know, I don't want to know, and I don't care.

At least, that's how I've always felt. But a part of me does wonder if maybe, just maybe, I do want to know the truth.

Not if it will hurt me, I remind myself.

But then, I can't imagine Mom would share anything about him if she thought there was a chance it would hurt. And still, I don't feel ready to look.

"Is he married?" I ask softly.

"No, honey," Mom assures me. "Never married."

That's one shoe that drops, and I feel something lighten in my chest. "Okay. That's good, I guess."

She nods. "Probably so. He never was the marrying kind."

Mom's eyes are closed, and her head's leaned back against the seat. The water that's supposed to soften and clean our feet is cooling, and a nail tech comes by to check the temperature.

"You ladies have the run of the place," she says. "Quiet day. You ready to start, or you want to soak a little longer?"

The woman puts a small squirt of lotion on her hands, rubs them together, then gives my mom a quick calf massage.

"Let's soak a little more," Mom says. "This is so relaxing. You mind, Lacey?"

I shake my head that I don't mind, and the lady washes her hands at a small sink behind the chairs. Then she fills both Mom's and my tubs with more hot water, lotions up her hands again, and rubs my calves gently but firmly while my toes soak.

I close my eyes and relax into the sensations. The hot, sudsy water. The gentle but firm touch of the nail tech. I feel loose and relaxed like a wet noodle by the time she stops. She taps my calf lightly and says, "I'll be back in just a few."

After she leaves, Mom breaks the silence. "Your dad rides a Harley."

My eyes fly open. "What?" I ask. "How do you know?"

She smiles. "He sent me pictures. Look through our messages."

I don't know if I want to, but I can't believe my dad rides a bike. Then I remember Mom telling me she dated a biker once.

"Who was the biker you dated?" I ask. "It wasn't Dad, was it?"

She shakes her head. "No. Your father was too broke to be a biker back then. But his best friend was. After your father left us, his best friend Eddie looked after me for a while. We went on a few dates, but it was nothing serious. I thought maybe he was snooping around for your dad, trying to find out if I planned on coming after him for child support or whatever."

That makes me sad. That mom would feel used by a guy that way. It makes me dislike my dad even more.

"But that wasn't the case at all," Mom says, her

voice cracking a little as she smiles. "Turns out, Eddie liked me a lot."

I shift in the chair to hear Mom's story better. Thankfully, only a few customers are filling the stations. They all have their heads bowed as they talk to their manicurists or watch the artistry as their fake nails are applied and decorated.

"Mom," I ask. "Was it real, then? The thing you had with Eddie?"

My mom sniffs, then lifts one shoulder as if to say who knows. "I had an infant, and I was alone, Lacey. I was vulnerable, and yeah, I guess I thought it was real. But I also knew, even when we were in it, that there was no way it could happen. Not for the long-term. Eddie was your father's best friend. He knew you were the reason your father bailed. Could you imagine a twenty-year-old guy trying to raise the illegitimate daughter of his best friend?"

Mom sighs.

"Those were different times. But I had fun. Eddie was a *lot* of fun." I throw Mom a look at the way she emphasizes "lot." She giggles. "No regrets here."

Then she rests her head back against the chair, and I admit, I'm tempted. Tempted to look at what my parents have said to each other. Mom's eyes are closed, but since I have her permission, I start with the messages.

I read from the top, so the oldest one. It looks like they have been friends for only a week or so. I always knew my dad's first name, but now I see it in black and white. Darnell Dennison.

I would never, ever have guessed that was his name. My mom always referred to him as Denny. Denny was never his first name at all.

I scroll through the messages, all of which are polite. Denny asked about me right away. But he didn't use my name.

Denny: How's your daughter?

Mom: She's amazing. Brilliant, beautiful. Lacey is the love of my life. Thanks for asking.

Denny: Lacey. Yeah. Of course she is. Good to hear.

Mom: I'm glad to see you're still in the union. Still working.

Denny: Yeah. Counting down the years until retirement. You?

Mom: Been with the same company over twenty years. Union where I'm at too.

Denny: Finally got that bike I was always dreaming of.

Then, a picture comes through. There's a bandanna on his head and sunglasses over his eyes, so it's hard to see him as the same man with the very outdated profile picture. But that's him. The man who made me then left me.

The original disappointing male.

I go back to Mom and Denny's exchange.

Mom: Well, isn't that gorgeous. Good for you, Denny. Be safe on that thing.

Denny: You know it. I'm in no rush to meet my maker.

Mom doesn't say anything, but then a second message from Denny comes through.

Denny: Maybe this is weird, but I'm glad you reached out. Thanks for connecting. I'm sorry, you know.

Mom: What for?

Denny: History. The past. I always knew I could never give you the fairy tale. And I knew that's what you wanted.

Mom: Well, my life's been really happy. No need to apologize now.

They don't chat anymore that day, and since I've seen all I need to see, I close the app and hand my mom back her phone.

"You're getting close with this Eagle guy," Mom says quietly. "I like him, Lacey," she adds. "I like him for you a lot."

I can't help but smile. "I like him too."

Mom nods. "Do you think he wants the same things you want?" she asks.

"Marriage, maybe kids, our own house with a yard for Ruby and all my future dogs?" I ask.

The truth is, I don't know. I know I haven't given up wanting the dream to come true, wanting that fairy-tale ending for myself.

But I'm unemployed, living with my mom, and I'm thirty years old. Life doesn't hand out golden tickets. And all the work I've done to make my own luck, I don't know what it's gotten me if the decisions I make in my personal life undo all the fruits of my labors.

The pedicurist comes back and asks who wants to go first. "You go ahead," I say to Mom. I close my eyes and picture Eagle. His tattoos, his bike, him in a tux. He's the man of my dreams. I'm sure of it.

But I've had so many dreams, and none of them have fully come true. Or if they have, they get stolen away in the snap of someone's fingers. Whether it's a lying boyfriend, a jealous wife, or a boss who would rather give up on me than fight for what's right, my brain refuses to believe that this thing with Eagle can have a happy ending.

Just as I'm thinking about him, my phone buzzes with a text. I pull my phone from my purse, and it's like the sun moves from behind the clouds when I read the message.

Eagle: Babe, Fingers said I shouldn't be at the mediation. Involved parties only, whatever the fuck that means. But I'm taking the day off work. I'm gonna be in the parking lot in my truck waiting for you the whole time. What time does it start?

I think this might be the longest text Eagle's ever sent me.

Me: Are you sure you want to be there?

Eagle: There for you the whole fucking time.

I send him a dozen kissy-face emojis, and to my absolute shock, he sends one back.

Me: Since when do you send emojis?

But in response, he just sends me one thing—a red heart.

CHAPTER 20
EAGLE

ONE MONTH LATER...

I wake up in Lacey's bed before sunrise. I hear her mom leave the house and lock up on her way to work. Tomorrow is the day Lacey's been dreading for a month. The mediation at the Lantana.

The last four weeks have passed in a blur. I somehow stuck it out with Crow, but I'm not on the demolition crew anymore. Crow's been teaching me tile-setting and flooring, and something about the precision and focus it takes to measure, plan, and cut the materials works for me. I can see patterns in it. I won't say I'm a corporate hack just yet, but I've been working steadily for the last month.

And that's suited me just fine. When I'm not on a job, I'm with Lacey, or Lacey and I are on the back of my bike, just exploring the parks and roads that bring me peace. I think they're starting to soothe her, too.

I'm lying on my side with my back to Lacey, so I quietly reach for my phone on the bedside table and check the time. It's way too early to get up, but I'm not going to be able to go back to sleep. I check to make sure my alarm's set, and then I set my phone down just as I feel a soft, naked body smush against my back.

"Can't sleep?" Lacey's voice is clear, like she's been lying awake for hours. "Me neither."

I roll to my back and pull her onto my chest. She rests her cheek against me and sighs. "Tomorrow's on your mind." I speak the words we are both thinking.

She nods lightly, the movement brushing her cheek against my chest. "I don't even know what to expect," she says. "I mean, I do. Fingers has prepared me, but I mean as far as the outcome. Once it's all over, it's going to be done. No more limbo. No more waiting while we swap letters through our attorneys. How do you let go of a dream?"

I grunt at that. I wish I had some advice for her. Some words that would ease what she's struggling with, but I don't know.

"It's been so long," I admit, my voice low, "since I've let myself have any kind of dream. I don't know how to hold on to one. I definitely don't know how to let go."

Lacey turns her face, and the breath slows in my chest. Even first thing in the morning, with her hair messy and lines from her pillow pressed into her cheeks, she is the most beautiful woman I've ever seen.

I smooth back her hair and just look at her, stunned and grateful. How is this woman mine?

"Eagle," she says softly, trailing her fingers through my chest hair. There ain't much there, but she loves to tease what I have. "Why don't you dream for yourself?

Isn't there anything you want so badly you keep going? Because you know, if you stop, what you love will slip away?"

I look away from her. I don't think we're talking about the same things. Lacey's dreams are for fancy weddings, high heels at work, and some job where she gets to do what she loves every day of her life. I'm more practical. I've had to be.

"Has there ever been anything that you've loved so much you couldn't stand the thought of losing it?"

When she puts it that way, yeah. There was. There is.

The bedroom is dark, but just enough early light is peeking around the curtains that I can make out Lacey's eyes as I talk. "I felt that way once about the club."

I tighten my arms around her, and she snuggles her head against me.

"I used to love the club," I admit. "The danger of what we did. Less you know, the better about that. Point is, I loved it. Whether we were riding out together or partying, I had purpose as long as I was a Disciple."

"And that's all changed?" Her voice is quiet, her hands still touching my skin but not moving.

"Yeah. Everything's different now." I wonder how much I can share with her. Wonder how much I should open up and reveal.

"Are you unhappy?" she asks.

"I was," I admit. "In a way. It's not that being straight wasn't for me. It's not that. It's the excitement. I don't get stiff in the dick over my work like some of these guys. They've all found other shit to do, and it seemed like I was the only one who missed the old ways. The way it used to be."

"I'm sorry," she says. "I never thought about it quite that way."

"Don't get me wrong, this is an easier life," I chuckle. "I don't worry about getting shot. I don't need to do time like Crow or get hurt. But I never really understood until recently how unhappy I was about the club changing."

I need something to do with my hands. I know what I want to say to Lacey. I know how it's gonna come out because I don't have a way with words. I gotta just say what's on my mind. And once I say it, there's no taking it back.

I stroke her hair once, then wrap my arms around her again, holding her close to my heart. I can feel the rhythm picking up, prodding me forward despite the fear. It's funny. I never felt fear riding into a conflict situation, facing down shit with my brothers at my side. But naked, holding the woman I know I can't live without, and standing on the edge of telling her how I feel, I'm fucking terrified.

"Lacey," I say, before I can chicken out of it. "Losing the Disciples was the worst thing that ever happened to me. I felt lost. Still do sometimes. But then you came along. Working with you was the best thing that ever happened to me. I lost the one thing that gave me purpose, but then I found a new, better purpose. My purpose now is you."

She stiffens under my hold, and I release her. I know I said too much. I know I fucked it up and pushed her away. It's too much, too soon. But I believe it. It's true, it's real, and if the last month of this thing with Lacey has taught me anything, it's that everything makes sense with her in my life. Without her, I go right back to feeling like nothing, no one. I hate it, but if she's gonna pull the rug out from under us, I want it to happen. I want it to happen now, not in three or six months when she figures out I'm not the fantasy.

"Do you really feel that way about me?" Her voice is reedy and thin, like she's trying to control her emotions.

"I do," I say simply. I don't apologize and I don't explain. She can kick my ass to the curb or ask me to leave. I'm prepared for it. In some ways, I've been waiting for it for the last month.

Lacey rolls away from me, sits up in bed, and covers her bare breasts with a sheet. Something in my gut churns, and I sit up too. Mentally, I'm thinking back to where I left my boots last night. My ass is naked, and I'll want to jump into my pants and boots with as much dignity as I can muster.

But instead of asking me to leave, Lacey takes my hand. "Thank God," she breathes. "Thank the good almighty saints and stars above."

Lacey isn't religious, so I snap a look at her. "Huh?" I ask. "What do you mean?"

She takes a deep breath. "I know we've known each other a long time, but all of this—" she sweeps a hand between us "—this is new, and it has me terrified."

I nod, ready for it. I'm not good enough. After a guy like Dylan, she needs someone more stable. Someone with a good job, someone who—

"I'm falling in love with you, Eagle," she blurts out.

"Come again?" I ask.

She shrugs, the sheet gripped between her hands. "I'm sorry if it's too much or too soon. But, Eagle, when I'm with you, I don't second-guess your every word. I don't doubt you, question you, or worry that somehow something I say is going to get twisted until I don't even know what I said anymore." She smiles but doesn't meet my eyes. "I always wanted the dream, but I think I was chasing it in all the wrong places. The universe had to put you in my face for two years before I finally got it. It's you. My dream man is you."

I take a minute to let her words sink in. I'm not sure I heard that right. I just told her she's my purpose, and instead of kicking my ass out of bed, she's falling for me.

I shake my head. "I'm not what you want, babe," I tell her. "I don't have a fancy house or a big bank account. I bounce between jobs and just barely stay out of trouble. And I mean just barely."

She nods. "I know who you are."

How can she know who I am? A man who's never been good enough for anyone. A man who's never really known who he was himself until maybe recently. Maybe he's still figuring himself out or figuring out who and what he wants to be next.

"I don't want you to feel trapped or rushed," she tells me. "Nothing has to change. I'm not asking for anything from you, Eagle. I just want you to know how I feel. About you."

Her words hit differently now that I realize she's not

about to break this off. I told her how I felt, and she wants me.

"So, what now?" I ask, clearing my throat. "I haven't had a conversation like this with a woman, maybe ever. Do we hug or something?"

Lacey starts laughing, and she drops the sheet, giving me an eyeful of her round, bouncing tits. "We could fuck," she says. "That's one fun way to seal the deal."

I shake my head. "I love fucking you," I admit.

Lacey climbs onto my lap, and I sit fully upright, leaning my back against the pillows.

"Eagle," she breathes my name into my neck. "You are so fucking delicious. I want to eat you."

She nibbles my neck, and it tickles so bad, I grab her wrists on instinct. She is cracking up, straining a little against my hold. "Hmm," she mumbles. "I like that. Maybe you can hold my wrists while I ride you."

I love that, and I watch wordlessly as she situates herself over my erection. She rests her weight lightly on me, then plants her palms on the wall behind me.

"Too awkward?" she asks. She's leaning toward my face, her arms just above my head, looking past her hard nipples and down into my face.

"I love my view," I tell her, reaching up and holding her wrists in my hands. "How's this?"

She moves her arms a little and I fight the movement, but it is, in fact, awkward.

"Let's try something else." I move quickly, still holding her wrists, and settle her on her back, lying down on the bed. Then I move her arms above her head and anchor her wrists against the mattress with my hands. "Too much?" I ask.

She shakes her head and parts her legs, making room for me to kneel between her thighs. "Perfect," she sighs.

I lean forward, putting as much weight as I think I can shift without hurting her into my hands. Then I roll my hips so my dick taps her opening.

"You're wet," I tell her, a grin claiming my face. I can't help it. Every time she's ready for me like this, with just a few kisses or touches, I feel like a god. She makes me feel like more than I am, more than I deserve to be.

"And horny," she breathes. "Now, fuck me hard."

Holding her wrists in place, I tease her clit with my cock, working my hips back and forth so I slide over her sensitive pussy. She's getting so wet, I slip inside her and quickly pull out, only to be met with groans and complaints.

"I forgot the condom," I tell her, releasing her wrists so I can reach into the bedside table for our stash. Once I'm sleeved, I grip my cock and center myself right over her wet pussy.

Her arms are still above her head, but before I take her wrists, I want to touch her, feel that drenched silk between her legs. The sun is coming up and filling the room with light, so I can see every pale hair on her arms, the pebbled texture of her hard nipples.

This woman is laid out, bare, and open for me. All for me. She is mine. And I'm going to make sure she never, ever questions that.

With my thumb, I stroke her clit, and I slip two fingers deep inside her. She moans and widens her legs, opening so I can watch as I enter her, watch as her clit swells with arousal. She works her hips, pressing her clit against my thumb, my fingers sinking deeper inside her.

"I want to come with you," she pants, but her words are thick and her eyes closed. She's lost in pleasure. And if I want it to be intense for her, unforgettable, I need to fuck her.

I yank my hand from her pussy and clamp both hands around her wrists, holding her securely against the bed. I slide my cock, slow and deep and hard until I can't go any farther.

"Fuck." She grinds out my name and thrashes against my hands.

"Tell me if you want me to let go," I tell her, and she nods, but I know she wants this. I can feel how turned on she is, how much she loves being fucked hard and fast.

I thrust inside her, deep and forcefully, and she gasps, whimpering my name. I use my abs to drive my body into hers, every thrust pushing her arms farther into the bed. Her tits, those glorious, gorgeous tits, bounce and shimmy with every thrust, moving back and forth, her nipples so hard, if I could stop fucking her, I'd stop only to suck those perfect copper peaks.

We're both moaning then, chasing a high that we want to drop from together. Me grinding into her, her grinding back, the breathless, senseless pleas between us bringing us closer and closer to the edge.

Finally, I hear Lacey's throaty cry, the sure tell that she's close, and her body tightens, her walls quivering and clamping down so hard on my cock that, even through the latex, I feel every spasm. I thrust harder into her, the combination of deep and wet, hard and tight impossible to resist.

I follow her over the cliff, panting and dripping sweat onto her bare breasts, shuddering and shouting her name as I release hot and frantic inside her. I don't roll away after I'm done but collapse on her chest like I love to do.

The sweat squishes between our chests, and my rapidly softening dick would fall out of her if she weren't still holding me so tight.

"Babe," she whispers. "I might come again." She wiggles her hips a little, using my body to stroke up against.

"I'm too soft," I say. "Give me a sec."

But she shakes her head. "I'm so, so close. I almost came again when you did. Suck my nipples."

My woman's wish is my command, so I rally the little bit of strength left in my wet sponge of a body, and I clamp my lips over her right nipple. I lick it lightly, just a warm, welcoming taste, until she moans and lets me know it's good. Then I suck hard, drawing the whole peak into my mouth and laving the hard tip with my tongue. I move my head, tugging the tender skin between my teeth, moving my face right to left until she's bucking wildly against me.

And before I know it, I'm hard again. I try not to think about what we're doing with the condom. It's still on, and I didn't get soft enough for it to slip off, so I give in to it. I fuck her, she fucks me, I suck her nipple, and within seconds, we're off to the stars again, screaming each other's names and coming in a blaze of sparks and stars.

When we're done, the alarm on my phone blares, jolting me out of the lust-filled haze.

"Perfect fucking timing," I laugh, pulling out of her and slamming a hand down on the device.

She moans a happy, satisfied sound, and I am pleased to see the condom is still in place. I don't know how, but my swimmers are contained. And I'm not even panicked. With any other woman, I'd be sweating bullets until I was sure not a single bit of my DNA made it out of that latex alive.

But with Lacey, I'm relieved but not nervous. I don't know what the future holds, but somehow, with her in front of me, I have purpose. With her beside me, I have strength. Whatever happens, I can almost dare to dream we'll be okay.

CHAPTER 21
LACEY

I CAN HEAR the water tinkling in the concrete fountain, but today, it doesn't fill me with the same sense of peace. I'm back at the Lantana, standing outside the front door, waiting for my lawyer to show up.

Big dark glasses cover my eyes, and I'm wearing my usual work uniform—a dark pencil skirt, a long-sleeved blouse, and sky-high heels. Today, I'm dressed in navy and light blue, a soft color that feels professional but not confrontational. I'm wearing my hair pulled back in a tight bun, and my signature red lipstick makes me feel a little like my old self.

I check my watch for the time and see that it's still early. I'm early. Old habits die hard, and I thought Fingers might want to brief me or something before we start. But the man I see coming up the walkway toward me isn't my lawyer. It's Dylan fucking Acosta.

I yank off my sunglasses so I can see him. "What the fuck are you doing here?"

"Lacey." The man has the nerve to lean in and try to kiss me, but I'm way too fast for that. I dodge him and back ten steps away. "Right," he says, pretending I haven't just rejected his petty attempt at a greeting. "Shame how things fall out sometimes." He pulls a phone from his pocket and starts tapping.

"Shame how things fall out?" I practically squeal it. "I'm here because of you. I lost my job because of you. Nothing fell out. You fucked me over."

Dylan hasn't bothered to look up from his phone, but he does turn at the dark shadow that rises up behind him.

"Hey, Lacey. You okay?" A deep, familiar voice fills my ears, and I can't help but start to breathe again.

Eagle is here. He kept his promise. Not that I doubted he would come, but he's not only here, he's being careful. Nothing he's said would give away the fact that we're dating. And while I don't care if Dylan knows, the less he knows about me and my life now, the better. Especially until this damn mediation is over.

Dylan shakes his head at Eagle. "I see you're not the only one who thought to bring witnesses." Then Dylan gives me a shit-eating grin and walks into the Lantana, calling behind him, "Good luck today, Lacey. You'll need it."

As soon as he's inside, Eagle steps a little closer. "Where the fuck is Fingers?" he asks. "Did you know that dickhead was going to be here?"

I shake my head. "If Fingers knew, he didn't say."

Just then, I see Fingers rushing up the walkway. He's got an old-school leather briefcase in one hand and a cigarette in the other. I almost ask him to stomp it out, but then I figure, screw it.

"Fingers," I call out, waving my hand.

He nods at me and extends the hand with the cigarette to Eagle in a weird half-wave kind of movement. "I'd shake, but I've got no free hands," he explains. "Sorry I'm late." He looks me over. "You look good. Good choice. Professional. Sedate. I forgot to tell you what to wear, but I figured you'd handle it."

Eagle is looking Fingers over skeptically. "What's going on, man?" he asks. "Fucking Acosta is here. He was just out here."

Fingers holds up his cigarette, takes a long final drag on it, then stomps it into the pavement. Fingers bangs a palm against his briefcase. "That's why I'm late. Counsel for the Lantana just disclosed to me this morning that he'd 'make a witness' available for questioning in case it helps the conversation."

"Is that normal?" I ask. "Shouldn't they have told us before this morning?"

"Not normal at all," Fingers says. "And I shot off a letter to document that I did not consent to the appearance of witnesses at a confidential, pretrial mediation." He sighs and pats his pocket where another box of cigarettes rests. "It's a little fuck-you to Lacey. The other side knows there's no reason to have a witness, and I won't let the man anywhere near the proceedings. Anything he says or hears could compromise what happens later if we end up in court." Fingers looks right at me. "They're trying to get to you, Lacey," he says. "They want you to feel bad, like you're in the wrong. In a meeting like this, I can't stop them from saying whatever they want, whether it's true or not, but your job is to stay calm, professional, and stick to the facts. No matter what the other side says or does."

My stomach sinks. Of course, Dylan would be here to shake my confidence. To make me question myself. Who I am and what I am worth.

During our entire relationship, he devalued me. Lied to me about his wife, his whereabouts. I don't know what else, and I don't want to know. All I care about is my future.

I want it all, and having it all means I have to start over. That means my time here as an event planner, in the beautiful, luxurious Villa Lantana, is really over. I don't think it hit me until today that this was inevitable. That there would be no going back.

But I see it clearly now, and I'm ready. Ready to fight for myself, for what's right, and for a new dream.

"I'll be out here the whole time," Eagle says. He moves toward me like he wants to kiss me, but he doesn't, and I understand why.

It's better that no one affiliated with the Lantana knows I'm with him.

"Thank you," I say, and then I turn to Fingers. "You ready?"

"Born ready," he says and holds the door of the Lantana open.

With my head held high, I set foot on the pink marble. I swallow my nerves and head for the last time ever into the conference room of the Lantana.

————

At seven o'clock, I text Eagle to please go home and eat. Tomorrow is Saturday, and he took it off as well, assuming we'd either be celebrating or drowning our sorrows. Either way, we planned to do it together.

Eagle: *You want me to wait at your mom's? How much longer?*

Me: *Mom's got book club at the house tonight. Unless you wanna talk about romance novels with the girls...*

Eagle: *I'm staying right here.*

I like his text and put my phone back on the conference room table. The two sides started out together, all of us except for Dylan in one room. The attorney for the Lantana made a little statement to the mediator. Nothing that happens today is binding unless we reach an agreement, but the mediator separated us after our opening statements so he could talk through the pros and cons of each side privately.

Just like Fingers said, the mediator trash-talked me a little. Nothing disrespectful, but he reminded me that a jury isn't going to look too favorably on a woman who dated a married man willingly, blindly for fourteen months. He reminded me of all the things I already know. That no one would believe that I didn't know he was married. He also reminded me that when jurors see pictures of Dylan with his gorgeous wife and his daughter on her wedding day, that again, I'm going to look like an untrustworthy homewrecker.

"There's two sides to this case," Fingers reminded me when I was at my lowest. Listening to all the arguments, all the ways I could be perceived as a terrible person, did get under my skin a bit. But then Fingers assured me, "Right now, that guy's in there telling Sergio he fucked up big-time. And he's explaining all the ways a jury isn't going to like that the Lantana rips off its customers and pressures its employees to sign big deals. Doesn't matter if it's true or not," he reminds me. "Juries like stories that make sense. And if you let both sides talk, we've both got stories that make sense. What we don't have is one right and one wrong. If we did, we probably would have settled already."

Fingers also tells me that dragging this out until we're hungry and tired is part of the mediator's strategy. They want to wear us down from our entrenched positions.

Finally, the mediator comes in with a huge smile on his face. "I think we've got a deal," he says. He's got a folded sheet of paper in his hand. "If I could get Ms. Mercer a job—a good job with comparable pay and benefits—and one month of pay as a bonus, would we have a deal?"

Fingers narrows his brows and looks at me. "You want a job, Lacey?"

I don't know what he means. "Here?" I ask the mediator. "A job with comparable pay and benefits here?"

He shakes his head. "Sergio has a property on the Gulf Coast. It's under construction now, but he's going to need a director of events. He's prepared to offer you that position, with no loss of seniority. Plus, one month of the salary you earned at the Lantana to help while you relocate. There will be a small budget for moving expenses on top of the already generous offer."

Already generous offer.

That's lawyer-speak for take this. It ain't gonna get much better.

I shake my head. "I'm not moving to Pensacola," I tell him. And I won't. Even if I didn't have Eagle, I won't leave my mom.

I ask Fingers if I can speak to him privately to consider the offer. The mediator leaves us, but he checks his watch. "I'd love to be able to get something inked before eight," he says, as if reminding us that we've been here since noon and haven't had anything but Lantana coffee and water despite the property having a full-service kitchen on-site.

Once the mediator leaves us, I point to my notepad. "This," I tell him. "This is what I want."

When the day started, I made a list for the mediator of the top ten things I needed to resolve this case today. I didn't have a top ten. I had five.

I wanted two years' salary paid to me in monthly payments for twelve months, starting the day we reach a settlement. That way, I'd technically have a year to find another job. I'd initially only wanted one year, but Fingers told me to double it because I have to expect to compromise from what I want to something I can live with.

I wanted my employment record to reflect that I'd resigned—not that I was terminated.

I wanted a confidentiality agreement in place so that

no one at the Lantana could speak about me, the Acosta incident, or the terms of my separation.

And finally, I wanted a written apology from Dylan Acosta for all the shit he'd put me through, which I knew would never happen, but a girl can dream.

I point to that list now. "What the fuck is going on, Fingers?" I ask him. "I said what it would take to resolve this case today. They offered me nothing on my list. I do not want to work with Sergio Lantana someplace else. Why? So he can fire me from there after this matter is resolved? I sure as hell don't want to move to Pensacola."

Fingers looks around at the no smoking sign on the wall for what must be the seven millionth time today. "Fuck it," he says, then pulls out his pack and lights up. He takes one drag, then pinches the end to put it out. "Smoke detectors in these places," he explains. Then he gets up and paces the floor. "We're almost done here," he says. "They are throwing out desperation offers, trying to get you to take something they want to give before they have to give in and eat shit."

He stops at the doorway and peeks out. Then he seems to get an idea. He opens the door and waves for the mediator to come back inside.

"So, I've talked to my client, and this—" Fingers shoves the written offer the mediator left with us back across the table "—this ain't gonna do it." He points to my list, specifically landing on that last item. "What do you say we get these two together, with counsel present, of course? Maybe an apology from Acosta would go a long way to showing my client that she needs to be a little more reasonable."

Fingers shoots me a look that is sharp, like he's disappointed in me. I gasp, immediately concerned.

"I'm sorry," I say, "I just thought—"

"Lacey, please." Fingers holds up a hand like he's exhausted and really doesn't want to hear it. "Let's see if Acosta is willing to apologize. If you get the most important thing on that list today, then maybe, because it don't cost nobody nothing, we'll move on to the other stuff."

The mediator looks at me, and I can't read what he's thinking, but I'll bet, based on what Fingers said, that he's going to tell Sergio and his attorney that I'm being difficult.

"Let me sort the issues out with the mediator, and we'll see if we can't get Dylan in here." Fingers follows the mediator out, and my stomach sinks.

But he's back in a minute.

As soon as he's back in his chair, I turn on Fingers, but he immediately holds a finger to his lips. "Shh," he hushes. "These walls got ears."

He leans close to me and whispers again, "You did good. Sometimes, you gotta help the other side think what you want 'em to think."

I sit back in my chair and try to figure out what he means. What good will it do for the mediator to think my own attorney is getting sick of me?

What feels like ten minutes later, there is a knock at the door. The mediator comes in, followed by the attorney for the Lantana, who I met this morning, and Dylan.

The mediator addresses me. "You're free to speak to Mr. Acosta," he says. "Both his and your attorneys will be right here. So please remember nothing you say is private and anything you do say could impact the direction of this case."

I nod and sit down in a chair. Dylan comes over and sits next to me. I cross my legs and move my chair a little closer to Dylan's. It's not because I want to cozy up to him, but I want to angle my face so all these people aren't just watching me. It feels weird.

And it must feel weird to Dylan too, because he starts to talk.

"It's nice not to be the one in the hot seat for once," he says with a wolfish laugh.

I frown and try to remember that we have an audience. I keep my tone even and my words simple. "It's definitely not a nice feeling," I say.

I flick a glance at him, and he's looking me over. "You were never tough enough, kiddo," he says. I never noticed how annoying it was that he called me that, but now, the term of endearment sounds tremendously patronizing. But I go with it.

"I know, I know," I say. "All I ever wanted was for people to have a happy event, an amazing fantasy. I wanted that for your daughter," I say. "I truly did, Dylan."

"I know you did, Lacey, but Olivia is a pain. She wants her pound of flesh." He turns toward me in his chair, and I almost fall out of mine.

"So, you're saying you know that I didn't try to sabotage the event? I didn't coerce you into spending more money—or really any of the stuff that Sergio is saying?" I make sure I sound like I'm blaming Sergio, not Dylan.

Dylan holds up his hands. "Are you seeing anyone, Lacey? How are you holding up without me?"

I resist the urge to roll my eyes and answer, knowing that my attorney and the attorney for the Lantana is right behind us. Not to mention the mediator.

"It's been hard," I say cryptically. "This has all been just so hard."

Dylan nods. "Well, I hope they do the right thing by you."

I furrow my brow in confusion because that's exactly what we're doing here, but Dylan seems completely oblivious to what's going on.

Then he claps his hands together and says, "So, when this shit's all over, call me. I miss you, Lace." He doesn't touch me, but he leans forward and says softly enough for me to feel like he's only talking to me but loudly enough for everyone else to hear it. "Olivia's going to Turkey again in the spring."

He doesn't complete that thought before he gets up and nods to the attorneys and mediators. "So, we talked. Are we good here?"

The mediator dismisses him, and both Fingers and the Lantana attorney step outside. What seems like half an hour later, Fingers comes back into the room alone, grinning like a cat that ate the canary.

"What the hell was that?" I ask. "I thought Dylan was going to apologize."

"You don't need that asshole's apology," he tells me. Then he grins again, lights his cigarette, takes a huge puff, and quickly extinguishes it. "When I went outside, I talked to the mediator. I told him not to tell Dylan he had to apologize to you. You're a sweet young girl whose heart got stomped on by the big, bad, rich guy." Fingers almost cackles, but the sound is silent. "I told the mediator I just thought you needed to feel like you'd mattered to Dylan. Like you weren't some piece of trash he'd thrown away as soon as Olivia was back from her Turkish vacation."

I'm completely confused. I don't understand how Dylan thinking I wanted validation from him—and not an apology—could work in my favor. So, I press Fingers on it. "Please dumb this down for me," I ask.

He nods. "Lacey, Acosta's got an ego the size of a stadium. Maybe bigger. A man like that won't apologize —he doesn't think he did anything wrong. But what he did just do is admit in front of a mediator, me, and counsel for the Lantana that he knows you did nothing wrong. None of the reasons the Lantana wants to fire you will hold water."

He waves a hand in the air.

"None of this is admissible, mind you. If we go to trial, we'll have to get him to say what he just said now on the record. And he won't. So, we'll be in a world of hurt later. But what we did accomplish is show that jerk-off counsel the kind of witness he's got. With the right pressure, Acosta will cave. Sergio will have nothing, and you'll look a whole lot better to a jury than the man who came to this mediation and made yet another pass at you."

I'm stunned.

Fingers, who looks more like a mob bookie or a gnome from a fantasy novel than an attorney, is a genius. I don't fully understand how he did what he did, but I know it works. Because a minute later, the mediator comes back in, his face grim and another piece of paper in his hand.

"Ms. Mercer," he says, "I think we have a deal."

CHAPTER 22
EAGLE

SINCE LACEY'S mom was hosting her monthly book club, Lacey followed me back to the compound. After the mediation, I got a short text saying, *We're done. Details when we're alone.*

I don't know what happened, and I'm itching inside, my skin feeling too hot and too tight at the same time.

I saw Fingers climb into his car and drive off, but he either didn't see me or pretended not to. Either way, with legal shit, I just followed their lead.

When we got to the compound, it was dead. Back in the day on a Friday night, the lot would have been overflowing with bikes and trucks, the main rooms stinking of beer and cheap perfume. Now, the compound is quiet except for the sound of a television coming from someplace.

I stand in the doorway and hold the door open for Lacey, who rushes in and throws herself into my arms.

"You okay?" I ask. That's my first question, and honest to fuck, it's the only one I care about. She could be fired, broke, and actually guilty of some of the stupid shit she's been accused of. All that matters to me is that she's okay.

She squeezes my waist hard, burying her face against my chest. She's quiet, but when she finally pulls back, the smile covers her entire face. "I'm amazing, babe," she says. "Amazing, but I'm also starving. And I need to call my mom."

She looks at her watch, then grimaces. "It's so late. Book club is probably over, and Mom's gotta be in bed already."

I nod. "Go to my room and put something on. I'll order food. You want Thai or pizza?"

"Surprise me," she says, then turns on her heel and almost walks right into Morris, the vice president of the club.

"Hey," I call out, surprised to see him here. I give him a hug and slap his back. "You in trouble with the old lady?"

Morris shakes his head, then gives Lacey a quick hug. "Hey, sweetheart." He sighs. "Alice and Zoey both came down with something today." He makes a horrified face, which means something to do with poop or puke. "Alice told me to save myself before I catch it, so I'm here for the night. I've got an on-site in the morning that I can't miss, but I'll take my chances at home after that."

He points to Lacey. "Make yourself at home. I'll be outta here in the morning."

Lacey thanks him, then heads off to my room to change. She's been keeping clothes and shoes here for the last few weeks, and I gotta say, having an old lady's stuff in my space doesn't feel confining like I once thought it would. It feels…good.

"I'm ordering food, man. You want anything?" I pull out my phone and open an app, while Morris sits down on a barstool at the kitchen counter.

"I'm good," he says. "And I know you got company, but you got a minute?"

I set my phone down, but Morris tells me to order, so I do, punching in a pizza order at one of our favorite places. "All right, brother. What's up?" I go around the counter to the fridge and grab two cold beers. I hold one out to Morris, who takes it.

"You been doing good on Crow's crew," he says. "You liking the work?"

I nod. "Took some getting used to," I admit. "But I'm settled in, I think."

Morris is quiet for a bit, like he's trying to make up his mind.

"Crow mention any problems?" I ask, concerned. Maybe I'm settling in all right but Crow's not liking the vibe, my attitude—anything could be wrong. And how the hell would I know? Maybe Crow asked Morris to sit me down. I can't imagine it'd happen this way, but since nothing's the way it used to be, I don't have a fucking clue what to expect.

I'm shocked at what Morris says next. "Crow thinks you need to run a crew, have more responsibility," he says. "You get bored and frustrated taking orders, but you're real good with the details."

I laugh. "I know that's true."

Morris nods and slides off his stool, the beer in his hands. "All right, then. Keep learning and figure out where you want to be. The contracting side is blowing up, so you want a crew, it's yours. You wanna learn design or something, we'll find a way."

He gets up and heads toward his office, but then he turns back and looks at me. "We ain't what we used to be," he says. "And I'd be lying if I said I didn't miss the old days sometimes."

I nod.

"You and I are more alike than you know," he says. "In five years, you might be running your own firm. Who knows? You've got it in you, Eagle."

That's as much of a pep talk as I've ever imagined getting from Morris, but it means a lot. I watch his back retreat as he walks down the hall toward his office. He's got a family now, and instead of running a criminal club, he's running a legit business. I know I haven't come around fast to all the changes, but I can definitely see the appeal.

I grab my phone and another beer, then answer the door when the pizza's delivered. All the while, Morris's words are echoing in my ears.

I've got leadership potential in me. The potential to run my own crew—or better, my own company.

I'm not gonna let myself get excited. The future is a long time off, and a lot can happen between now and then. What I do know is there's a gorgeous woman waiting in my room, a hot pizza in my hand, and two cold beers getting warmer by the minute.

I head into my room and find Lacey sitting on my

bed. Her hair is loose from its bun, and she's barefoot and braless. She's wearing a pair of my boxers and one of my tank tops. The neck and sleeves are so big on her, I can see almost every inch of her tits.

"Uh, pizza's here," I say. "But you look like you're trying to distract me from eating it."

She jumps up and grabs a beer, bouncing on her toes as I set the pizza on a side table. "I'm just happy," she says. "So, so happy." She runs her free hand along her body. "And I like wearing your clothes. I feel closer to you that way."

I set my beer on the dresser and open my arms. "Tell me," I say. "What happened today?"

She kisses me. "I will," she promises. "But babe, I got to eat."

We grab slices of pizza and sit on my bed, Lacey explaining how the day unfolded while we eat. By the time we've finished two slices of pizza and both beers, I feel like I've heard everything about the entire eight-hour experience. Except, of course, for the ending.

"So, then," Lacey says, shifting on my bed, her tits falling out of the sides of my tank, "they gave me almost everything I wanted, Eagle."

I don't know what that means, so I ask her. "A job, money? What, babe? What does that mean?"

"I did not get an apology from Dylan, but I wasn't expecting that anyway. But Sergio agreed to pay me not quite the full two years of salary but eighteen months, plus they will pay for my health insurance during that time, so worth almost more than two years' salary. That was Fingers's idea," she adds. "He's smart."

I nod, thrilled to hear the club's attorney lived up to his reputation.

"And my separation will be categorized as a voluntary resignation," she says. "No firing or termination on my record."

I'm confused. "So, they're going to pay you not to work there and to tell anyone who asks that you left willingly?"

She nods. "And we are all bound by a basic confidentiality agreement. They can't stop the employees from gossiping, but at least if anyone who might try to hire me inquires, they'll get an official story from Lantana management that doesn't make me sound like a brazen ho."

I laugh out loud at that. The last thing anyone would think Lacey is would probably be a brazen ho. But I'm happy there is some confidentiality built into the agreement.

"But you can't tell anyone," she says quickly. "That could compromise the agreement."

I pretend to zip my lips. "Don't know a thing about it," I joke.

Full and sleepy, Lacey yawns. "Eagle, do you know what this means?" She climbs under the covers, not even bothering to brush her teeth.

I'm still dressed, but I climb in beside her. "What, babe?" I ask.

"I have two years to find a new dream," she says quietly. "Something that's going to last. Maybe something that no one can ever take away from me."

My bed, a double, is smaller than the queen Lacey

has in her room. It's tight sleeping here, but I love being close to her.

I love Lacey. And after only one month, I'm not ready to tell her. But I think I have to start admitting it to myself.

"Morris wants me to find a path on the crew," I tell her. "Looks like we're both building new dreams."

Lacey closes her eyes and pats her rear end. "Spoon me," she says softly, burying her face in the pillow.

I get out of bed and drop my clothes to the floor. I demolished more of the pizza while she was talking, and the rest, I'll toss. I don't want to leave her side even to put what's left in the fridge.

Once I'm down to my birthday suit, I climb under the sheet and snuggle tight against Lacey's ass. My cock jerks at the contact.

"You wanna sleep, babe?" I ask.

"For a second," she murmurs. "But then wake me up."

I'm not sure she means it, but I lie there awake, my cock throbbing against her ass, just thinking of the many ways I'd love to keep her from sleeping.

But pretty soon, her breaths sound heavier, and my eyes itch. I close them only momentarily, but before I know it, I fall sound asleep.

———

I wake up to the sound of angry knocking at my bedroom door. I don't even have a chance to cover my dick before the door flies open.

"What the fuck?" I yell, my first thought to grab the sheet and cover Lacey.

It's sunny outside, but I was in such a deep sleep, I don't have a clue what time it is. When I shout, Lacey rolls on to her side, squinting her eyes open.

"Eagle?" she mumbles, her hair tangled and her breasts falling out the side of my tank when she sits up. "Is everything okay?" She covers herself with the sheet.

I'm hopping out of bed, jumping around on one foot to try to pull a pair of pants on over my ass. "Get out," I say angrily. "Just get the fuck out."

I never lock my door. Have no need. Some of the other guys do, but I never have guests over. And any of my brothers who open my door when it is closed know they'll get their dick chopped off.

There's only one person who would storm into my room like this, and she ain't supposed to be here.

I lock my gaze on Lacey as she looks from me to the woman standing in my doorway.

"Eagle?" Lacey asks again. "What's happening?"

"Aw, she's fucking cute, Eagle." The woman in the doorway, my bitch of a wife, Linda, purses her overly glossy lips and makes a face. "Ain't she a little young for you?"

"Linda," I seethe. "Get the fuck out of my room."

She crosses her arms over her chest and glares. "If you'd ever answer a fucking phone, I wouldn't have to come down here like this. You gave me no choice, Eagle." Linda's loud voice pierces the quiet of the compound.

The next thing I know, I hear heavy footsteps in the hall. "What the fuck's going on?"

"Tiny!" I yell. "Get this bitch out of here."

"*Linda.*" I hear Tiny, but then I see him. He's standing behind Linda, blocking her from leaving. "You know I don't wanna lay hands on a woman, but you're outta line."

Linda slaps Tiny on the shoulder and scoffs. "Give me a fucking break, Tiny. It wasn't that long ago you let me suck you off while this one watched." She jerks a finger at me. "You think him fucking around with some bitch is front-page news? I don't give a fuck about this chick. I need to talk to my goddamn husband."

The word comes out and lands hard. I feel it, like a fifty-pound weight dropped on my chest.

And I literally hear the air leave Lacey's lungs.

"Linda, you gave shitty head, and that was about a million years ago." Leave it to Tiny to focus on the real problem here. "Now, I'm not gonna ask you again. You got business with Eagle, you take it up with him privately. Not here. You were banned from the compound, if I remember correctly, and that's a ban for life. Now get the fuck out before I move your ass myself."

Linda turns and looks at Lacey, then me, a patronizing smile on her overly tanned face. "Eagle, dear," she says, her voice saccharine sweet. "I'll be waiting outside. And if you're not out there in five minutes, I'll slash your fucking tires." She gives Lacey a shitty grin. "The local cops won't prosecute property damage under a grand, so I'll only slash three of them." She flashes a small knife she's carrying in her purse as if to prove she'll really do it.

Then she huffs and stomps past Tiny.

Tiny watches her walk away, then looks from me to Lacey and back. "Jesus fuck, that woman," he says, shaking his head. "I'll follow her, but I can only buy you five minutes, tops."

He slams my bedroom door closed, leaving me alone with Lacey.

"Lacey," I say, yanking a T-shirt over my head. "Let me explain."

"You're married," she says, her face white as a sheet, her voice flat. "That was Linda. You're married to Linda."

Goddammit, I should have covered that tattoo years ago. I should have dealt with Linda years ago. My whole life is collapsing into a pile of should-haves right now.

"Lacey, you gotta understand. We've been married for over twenty years—"

"Twenty years," she echoes, looking less pale and more green as she covers her mouth. "I think I'm gonna be sick. I'm so sorry."

She scrambles out of bed, but I grab her arm. "Lacey, for God's sake. Please. It's not like what happened with Dylan. I didn't lie to you. We haven't been together in years. She came down here because I won't talk to her. We don't even see each other."

"You know what happened with Dylan," she says, "and you're married."

My heart is thundering in my chest, but even though

I know Linda may be out there slashing my tires or tearing into Tiny, I cannot let Lacey go.

I cannot let her leave. Not like this. Not without knowing the whole story.

"Lacey, please. Please let me explain."

I think of all the times that we lay in bed just talking. She told me about Dylan over many talks, sometimes making fun of herself for her innocence, for being so oblivious. Other times, she beat herself up so hard, I held her while she cried.

Over the last month, Lacey has been nothing if not open. And I've been nothing if not careful. Guarded. Maybe even deceptive.

But I can't tell her the whole story, no matter how badly I want to. Not now. Because Lacey runs off to the bathroom and locks herself in.

CHAPTER 23
LACEY

ONCE I STOP THROWING UP, I take a hot shower. I sit in the bathroom in the compound, wrapped in a towel and shaking from head to toe. I don't want to leave this room. Don't want to listen to excuses or stories. I definitely don't want to listen to any lies.

I want to sneak into Eagle's room, get my clothes and purse, and run. I rinse my mouth for the millionth time under the faucet then pray there is nothing else my body plans to do to reject the situation I'm in. I threw up until I coughed and dry-heaved, so my stomach is empty.

But my heart is overflowing with tears, and soon enough, I'm gonna lose what's left of my composure. But at least I think I can leave here without puking all over my own shoes.

I think I might be in shock, so I take this moment to tiptoe down the hall. Eagle's door is open, so I slide inside, lock the door, and try to put my clothes from yesterday back on. But slipping on my skirt makes me feel all the more miserable. Just last night, I was flying high. Drunk on possibilities and maybe a little drunk on cheap pizza and beer. But I didn't care. I was happy. I had hope for a future. For a future with Eagle. New dreams, new plans.

And now, all I can see is how I've fucked up... Again. I trusted a man who, by all means, I should have dug into. It's not like Dylan didn't just happen. He did. And yet, here I am again.

As I frantically gather everything I've left over the past month in Eagle's room—my toiletries, my clothes, extra chargers for my devices—my mind races. If I were still employed at the Lantana, I could look back at his employment paperwork. I could see who his emergency contact is, see what he put on his tax forms for his deductions.

But none of that is accessible to me anymore. And it doesn't matter. None of it matters. I let Eagle into my bed, my heart, my home, and he lied to me. Just like all the others.

I realize, if Linda is talking to Eagle in the parking lot, I have to walk right past them to get to my car. The thought sends a new wave of nausea rocketing through my stomach, but I take a deep breath. I haven't done anything wrong. I, again, was simply too naïve and stupid, blindly trusting the man I was seeing.

I, again, fucked up. But that doesn't mean I can't hold my head high as I walk past Eagle...and his wife.

Now, the tears are falling, burning the backs of my

eyes and nose, but I can't stop them. And I won't try. I don't care.

I hold my heels in my hands, and all my other shit is gathered in my arms. I unlock Eagle's room and pad through the compound in my bare feet. When I get to the main door, I slip into my shoes and lift my chin, only to hear a throat clear behind me.

"That one's a piece a work."

I turn to see Tiny sitting at the kitchen counter, a giant insulated glass with a reusable straw in front of him. It's early, only nine in the morning by my watch, but I've seen Tiny put down a half gallon of soda first thing in the morning like some people drink water.

"Tiny, I need to go," I tell him.

He nods, waving at the door. "I ain't stopping ya," he says simply. "But it'd be a shame if you didn't give Eagle the benefit of the doubt. Not a lot of people have. And he's pretty fucked up, in case you didn't notice."

That catches my attention. My stomach is empty, and my mouth still feels sour, but I juggle all my shit and walk toward the kitchen.

"What do you mean, he's fucked up?" I ask.

Tiny shrugs. "We all get put through the wringer by life. But Eagle? It's like rinse and repeat with that guy."

Tiny takes a huge sip of his drink, then belches loudly. "Excuse me," he says. "It's fucking early, and my system doesn't like waking up this early for anything other than my grandkid."

He pats the stool next to him. "Sit a minute. I'm not going to stop you, though. You want to go, you know the way out."

I swallow hard and set down my things on the counter, but I don't sit. "He lied, Tiny. He's married. He lied to me over and over and over."

Tiny snorts. "Did he? I mean, maybe leaving out the shitty chapter of his life that was Linda wasn't a smart move, but she ain't no wife."

I start to protest, but Tiny holds up a hand. "Lemme tell you a story. It'll take five minutes of your time. Then you wanna leave, you think Eagle's a lying loser, I'll hold the fucking door for you. Even carry your shit to your car."

I nod, and then I wait. "Okay. I'll listen."

I can't imagine what Tiny could tell me that could ease this pain. That could take away the dishonesty, the hiding, the lies that Eagle has told—maybe not directly, but has he lied by omission? By leaving out critical information? Yeah. Yes, he has. He's lied. And I don't know how to rebuild trust once it's been broken.

Tiny takes a deep breath, then sighs. "Once upon a time, this club was a very different place." He grins as he says it, like he's talking about an old friend. "The Disciples were feared, Lacey. And you know why we were feared? We did bad, bad shit. Guns, drugs, women —you name it, we dabbled.

"But a skinny young prospect has to prove himself, has to earn his way into the brotherhood. I'm not saying we're angels by any means. But we do have a code. When Eagle started fucking Linda, they were stupid kids. He was fucking three or four other bitches. I don't even remember now who they were. But Linda, she comes running into the club crying that she's late, she's late.

"Now, I tell Eagle what I would do, and this is what I did plenty of times with women who tried to land a Disciple the shady way. I said, you wait till she's showing. Then, when the kid arrives, you get a paternity test. Then, and only then, do you decide if you're gonna be a father."

The similarities between Tiny's approach and what my dad did make the room nearly spin. I clutch the counter and hope he's almost done. "But not Eagle. That's not what he did. Linda comes bellyaching in one day, claiming she's late, and this guy panics. Decides he's got to do the right thing. So, he hasn't got a pot to piss in or even a full patch yet, and the asshole marries her. And guess what? Six weeks later, no baby. Was there ever a baby? Who knows. Anybody's guess. But Eagle had a bigger problem on his hands than a kid. He had himself an old lady."

I hear the front door open, and I hope it's not Eagle coming back, but it is. I can tell from the way his boots hit the floor that he's rushing.

Tiny turns on his stool and meets my eyes. "You know what's real hard to do?" he asks. "Divorce a woman who tried to use you. And when you've got no legitimate income on the books for most of your adult life…" He makes a tsking sound and shakes his head. "It's real hard to find a claim for no alimony when you have a five-figure bike, a truck, and all kinds of shiny devices, but no legal, verifiable source of income."

He climbs down from his stool and gives me a nod.

"See you around, Lacey." Then he walks away, leaving me and all my shit in the kitchen.

Eagle comes into the kitchen, his face red and flushed, his eyes wide and concerned. "Lacey," he says. "Can we talk, please?"

I don't really want to talk about anything else, not here, not like this. I need time alone. I need time to think.

But Eagle's looking at me with such pain in his eyes. He looks on the verge of tears.

"I just want to ask a few questions," I say. "Is that all right?"

He nods. "Anything, yes. I'll answer anything. Do you want to go to my room? We can—"

I shake my head. "Here, please. If we go to your room, I'll just want to hug you, and..." My voice breaks. "I can't do that right now."

Eagle swipes a fist at his eye and nods. "Ask anything. Anything you want to know."

I don't even know where to start, but I start with the obvious. "How long have you been married?"

"Since I was twenty," he says, his voice flat. "So, twenty-four years."

I almost topple off the kitchen stool. Eagle has been married for almost as long as I've been alive. "How long has it been since you were intimate with your wife?" It kills me to ask. My voice cracks on the word "intimate," but I need to know it. I absolutely need the truth.

"Twenty years," he says, his voice a low rasp. "She's hooked up with Tiny more recently than she has me, and she's been banned from the club for years. But to answer your question, twenty years."

I'm not sure if that answer makes me feel better or worse, but I go on. "Are you ever going to get divorced?"

He nods, his bright-blue eyes never leaving mine. "Yes."

I have so many questions burning through my mind right now, I can't think of what to ask next. Why hasn't he already, when will he, why didn't he already, but then I just feel stupid. Childish. Maybe Tiny is right. Maybe it's hard to do things by the book when you don't live by the book. But I can't believe, even if all of this is true, if he plans to divorce Linda someday, why he wouldn't at least tell me? Give me the option of understanding his story and making decisions based on truth. He deprived me of that. Whether he meant to or not. I don't know if I care if Eagle *was* a criminal. If he did bad things in his past.

I'm his present, and I thought he was my future.

He should have told me.

"What else?" he asks, his voice tight.

I look away from him. I don't know what to do now, what to say. I thought I was falling for Eagle—I was. I was falling for Eagle. But I can't build new dreams with old behaviors. I can't. I just can't.

"Thank you for explaining," I say, then I climb off the stool and start to gather my things.

"Lacey." The way he says my name sends my heart into overdrive. He sounds like he's breaking. Like he's as broken inside as I am. "If you're going to leave, will you at least let me say a few things that you didn't ask about?"

I look down at my clothes, my toothbrush, my charging cables. All the small things that blend together when you want to make a life with someone. If only it was as easy as picking up our stuff and moving on.

I shouldn't listen. Shouldn't give him the chance to tell me any more lies, but I have to. If all he has to give me are more lies, I'd rather know it now and shut that door forever.

"What is it?" I ask, trying to hold my voice steady.

Eagle doesn't touch me, but he comes close. "You know how I feel about you, Lacey," he starts. "And if you don't, I'll tell you. I'm fucking crazy about you. Use whatever fancy term you want. You're mine, and all I want is to be yours."

I break then, a sob slipping past my lips, but he continues.

"I didn't tell you about Linda because, and I know this sounds fucking stupid, she means nothing to me. Not in the way fucking Acosta says his wife doesn't mean anything to him. I mean that Linda and I are married on paper. But now, she wants a divorce. That's what she's been hounding me for. I know that means a lawyer and dredging up my financial records, dividing our property. And I don't want that woman digging into anything that I've built in my life. Not one goddamned thing. That woman tore me down every way she possibly could. Fucked anything at the club that moved. Tiny, Morris, strangers, rival clubs—it didn't matter. If it had a dick and that dick was even halfway hard, Linda got on it."

He shakes his head. "And I wouldn't care if that bitch let every cock in the state of Florida inside. What mattered is that when we were young—when I still believed that she married me because she wanted me, not because she had to or she thought she had to—she hurt me in ways I can't describe.

"She made me believe I was worthless. That I was the reason she fucked around. That I was the reason she didn't want me. That I was the reason she lost the baby we sure as hell didn't mean to make, but it was ours. And all of it was my fault because I was not good enough. And maybe I heard enough of that from my old man or from teachers or from fucking life, but I believed her."

Eagle is moving away from me now. As if now that he's shared so much, he can't bear the thought of me seeing him.

I let him go. I have to.

He doesn't say anything more, his breaths coming hard and fast. Once it's clear he's calm, he says one more thing.

"You, Lacey. You were the first thing in twenty years that made me believe in myself. That made me believe I was more than the worthless trash I've been all this time. You, Lacey. You talk about your dreams and your fantasy life, your dream job and your future. I never even let myself hope for any of that shit. Not until you."

He's backing away now, walking toward the door to the compound.

"And I'm sorry if I was too chickenshit to tell you the one thing I knew would prove beyond a doubt that I'm not good enough for you. Yeah, I have a wife. But you, Lacey, you're the love of my life."

I swallow back my sobs, thick, hot tears coating my cheeks. I sniffle and wipe the back of my hand against my nose. "I have to go," I tell him. I gather up my things and stumble on my heels toward the door. I try to get past him, but he stops me with a hand.

"Lacey," he whispers, his voice a ragged, broken plea. "Please don't leave me."

I almost scream, the sound I make so animalistic and raw, I can't believe it comes from my throat.

Then I kick off my shoes, yank open the door, and run.

CHAPTER 24
EAGLE

TWO MONTHS *later*

It's pretty unbelievable what money and a decent attorney can accomplish. Over the last two months, Fingers has buried Linda in paperwork. First, the petition for dissolution of our marriage.

Yeah, finally, after far too long, it wasn't her who filed for divorce—it was me.

After that, Fingers sent over a lot of demands for documents. Since Linda's attorney demanded alimony and disclosure of marital assets and all other kinds of shit, Fingers did the same. And worse, he sent over a request that Linda formally disclose all the people she fucked while we were married. I knew of at least eight, but given how long we'd been apart, just making that demand would send her temper through the roof.

I haven't exactly been celibate, but Fingers had a theory that if we told Linda we were going to try to prove infidelity, and that we might seek out sworn statements from some of the men she slept with in the early years before I finally gave myself free rein to get what I could... Well, she might just back off on the demand for money.

It's not over yet, and from what Fingers tells me, it could be a long and painful battle. Not to mention expensive. But it's done. The process has started, and there's no going back. Someday, I will be a single man. Well, I'll be free of Linda. Let's put it that way.

I sincerely hope that I won't be single for long.

I haven't texted, called, or even seen Lacey—other than the social media stalking I've done. She doesn't post often, but every time she adds a goofy picture of Ruby or posts the cinnamon raisin bread her mom's brought home from the bakery, I feel a little less dead inside.

Lacey is still out there in the world. Beautiful, quirky, dreamer Lacey. She may not be mine now, but I haven't given up. That's something she taught me. To believe in my dreams and hold on so tight that even when they seem out of reach, never, ever lose faith.

Someday, when I have my shit together, I'm going to find her. Tell her everything I've done to deserve her. It may not be enough, and I know that. Too little, too late, and all that shit. What matters now is that I'm doing it. I'm fixing my life, my heart, and I'm building the faith in myself that I've been missing for too long.

"Yo, asshole." I hear Crow's voice on the other end of the walkie-talkie. He's on the third floor of a small private school where we're bidding out the renovation of all of the bathrooms. It's a huge job, and if we get it, this summer when school's out, I'll be in charge of a massive project. A crew of my own.

"What's up?" I ask, clicking the button to talk, then releasing it to listen.

"You've got a free morning tomorrow. I've got a property that needs an estimate. You wanna go, or should I send Morris?"

I've been taking every project Crow's sent my way, working late nights, weekends, whatever he needs. I need every spare penny to pay Fingers's legal bills, and I want to save what I can for whatever comes next.

"I'm on it," I tell him. "Send the details to my phone."

I head out to my truck and check my phone for the millionth time. I have the usual work emails—messages from Morris and Tiny, Crow and Arrow—but no texts. Nothing from Lacey. I haven't texted her either, but I can't. I need to be ready when I see her next.

I need to be perfect.

I put the address for the meeting tomorrow into my GPS and head back to the compound. I'm tired, hungry, and in need of a shower. Just like every other day since Lacey left. Wash, rinse, repeat. But somehow, I don't get bored or resentful. I don't miss the old days the way I used to. Maybe all I really needed was a goal I gave a shit about. Now, I have so many goals, I've started keeping track of them.

The only one I don't know if I'll ever accomplish is getting Lacey back. But it's top on my list and always will be. Always.

————

The next morning, I arrive at the job early. The office of the nonprofit organization that wants the estimate is located in a house that's been renovated and zoned for commercial use. It's badly in need of repairs. I can see from the street that the shutters are peeling. The wood frame is warped. The concrete path is pockmarked and broken in places—signs of the ground settling and overall disrepair, making the place look absolutely depressing.

I mentally start doing calculations in my head as soon as I ring the bell on the front door. A receptionist calls out through a video doorbell, the most new and functional thing I've seen so far.

"Good morning. Can I help you?"

"Yes, ma'am. Good morning. I'm here to provide an estimate. I'm Logan Taylor's foreman."

I always chuckle when I say Crow's real name. But if it sounds funny to the receptionist, she doesn't show it. She buzzes me into the front door, which closes and locks behind me.

The girl who greets me is pretty in a plain way, and she has a nice smile. But her eyes aren't as bright and deep as Lacey's. She's wearing a skirt, but not a pencil skirt. Her hair, though it's in a bun, isn't the tight, low bun that used to sit at the nape of Lacey's neck.

I miss her. That's the God's honest truth. I'll never stop missing her.

"Our executive director will be right with you," the receptionist says. She offers me a chair, but the "chair" is a folding chair. I don't know what half of the things I'm looking at are used for, but this seems to be a place where a lot of equipment comes to die.

Before I can even sit, another woman comes rushing into the room, her hand extended. "Hi there," she says, giving me a huge smile. "I'm Susan Leach, Executive Director. Thanks so much for coming. There's a lot to do here, and I'd like you to meet the team so we can go over our goals and our budget before you get started looking around."

I shake Susan's hand and introduce myself. "I'm Easton Wilson," I tell her. "But my friends call me Eagle."

"Eagle?" she asks, giving me a funny smile. "Well, that's a terrific name. I'd like to use that one, if you don't mind. Now, follow me."

She leads me through the house that has been converted to make the living spaces on the first floor into work nooks. The place is cluttered, books and marketing materials with kids in hospitals and home settings on the covers scattered everywhere. I follow her past what was once the kitchen of this house, but which is now clearly an office kitchen. Coffee mugs labeled with blue painter's tape line the counter, and I can see cans of soup and other dry goods left out for communal snacking. In some ways, this place reminds me a lot of the compound.

As Susan takes me toward the central staircase, I can already tell there's no way a nonprofit has the funds to redo this place. The floorboards creak, I smell mildew that no doubt means water damage, and cosmetically, this place needs to come down. All the medical equipment lodged against walls and blocking walkways has to be violating at least ten city codes.

Susan heads down a hallway and stops in front of an open door. She knocks lightly, and a woman shoves a pair of glasses off her nose to get a better look at us.

"Yes? Susan, what is it?"

I recognize that woman, but it takes me a minute to remember from where. But it takes her half the time to recognize me.

"Well, I'll be darned." Danielle, Lacey's mom's friend, stands from her chair. "Great to see you, Eagle."

She holds a hand out to me, and I shake it. "You came highly recommended," she says. "Have a seat."

Susan, the executive director, and Danielle both sit. I wedge myself into a slightly nicer wooden chair that's close to Susan's. These people must not get a lot of visitors. I have to shift my chair until it's almost touching Danielle's desk so I'm not knee-to-knee with Susan.

"So, Eagle," Danielle says with a bright smile. She waves a hand around the office. "I wear about three hats here at Gabriel's Closet, and that's two hats too many."

She goes on to explain how the nonprofit just recently lost its lease on a different building due to a huge spike in the rent. But Danielle's parents recently moved to Nevada to be closer to their grandchildren and offered the converted house where they used to operate an insurance agency to the nonprofit for a steal.

"So, here's my dilemma," Danielle says. "My parents sold me this house, which thankfully is zoned for commercial use. But we connect children in need with medical devices and equipment. We get a lot of donated items that are large and which need to be kept securely stored for weeks, sometimes months, until we find a child who needs it." Danielle explains a little about their business, but I am curious why I am here. "That's where you come in," she says. "I fundraise, do the books, run the marketing that we do—what little we can do." Her eyes meet mine, and she smiles softly. "We have taken on a brilliant intern. She's helping me with every aspect of my job, and it's my hope that we can offer her paid work in the coming year or so. But for now, we need an addition built on to this house. One that is accessible for clients who are able to get to us, and one that can safely store the equipment we take in."

She explains that they have an architect on the board of directors who is willing to donate plans, but she needs a contractor to build the addition. She opens a drawer in her desk and shows me some rough draw-ings—not the architect's images, but the hand-drawn sketches she'd probably shown the architect.

"We'd love to get a bid from you for the work," Danielle says.

Susan speaks up then. "We'd also like you to meet our intern since one of her responsibilities will be to coordinate with whatever contractor we choose. She'll essentially be a project manager of sorts."

I nod. "Happy to help. Can I take a look at those?" I lean forward and start looking over the specs, mentally calculating exactly the kind of structure they need.

Danielle gets up from behind her desk and heads

toward the door while I'm studying the drawings. When I turn to look behind me and ask a few questions, my heart slams to a halt in my chest.

"Lacey." I say her name like it's the last word I'll ever speak. I savor it. I breathe it in. She's here.

I climb out of the tight space the chair is wedged into and stand.

"Eagle," she says softly. "Thanks for coming. I honestly wasn't sure if they'd send you." She bites her lower lip. "That's not entirely true. I wasn't sure, but when I called, I did ask Crow to send you."

She smiles and looks down at her feet. She's wearing jeans and running shoes, the pencil skirt and heels gone. The ruby-red lipstick and tiny bun are still there, though. Her power outfit, just powering a different kind of work.

"I'm cleaning and moving equipment today. We just got in a bath chair and swing that were used by a teenager. It's a lot of hosing down and sterilizing." She shrugs. "I'm dressing for the job I have, not the job I want. But that will come soon enough."

If she feels anything seeing me, she doesn't give it away. There is a soft flush on her cheeks, but she's not meeting my eyes.

I don't know what to say. I just have one question. "Will you be my boss again?"

She laughs then, a sudden, sparkling sound. "No." She shakes her head. "I'm just an intern. While I'm deciding what my next move is, I'm learning a totally new industry. Fundraising and development, marketing..." She holds up her hands. "It's a nice change, learning rather than managing."

"You've gone from riches to rags," I say. "Are you happy here?"

She looks thoughtful. "I never thought about it that way. You're right. This is a riches-to-rags story." She nods. "But I like it. It suits me and where I am right now. I'm happy here. I used to get up every morning and savor the beauty of the place where I worked. The magic of the events was just dreamy. I could get lost in the fantasy, even though I knew it wasn't real."

She rubs her face and finally, finally meets my eyes. "Now, I wake up with a different kind of purpose. What we do here isn't glamorous. It's dirty, physical work. But it's real. It matters to a lot of people. And I've met some of the most amazing people I've ever met in my whole life. Parents, clients." She smiles. "I am happy here. It's just a different kind of happiness."

I understand that. I've felt the same way since losing Lacey. I can't say I'm happy without her, but life, my work... It all hits differently now. I have purpose, and I'm okay with it.

"So, I won't be working for you," I clarify.

"No, but you'll be working with me. We'll be equals. Peers," she says with a smile. "And no one can really get mad if we are more than just coworkers because, you know, no conflict of interest. I have no power over whether you get this contract." She shrugs. "I'm not even getting paid. Unpaid intern at thirty years old."

I don't care whether she's making minimum wage

or stripper quantities of cash. All I heard was *more than coworkers*.

"Lacey." I reach for her, sliding a hand behind her neck. Then I catch myself and step back. "Sorry," I say. "Old habits. I shouldn't. We're at your work."

I take three steps back, but then Lacey surges forward and throws herself into my arms.

"I miss you so much," she whispers against my shirt. "God, Eagle. I…"

I hold her tight, my arms trembling, my chest heaving. I can't say anything. Won't say anything. I don't want to fuck this up. And yet, I believe she cares about me. I believe that what we have means more than anything else in my life. I have to believe she feels it too.

"I fucked up, but I love you. I'm willing to work as long as it takes and wait as long as you need for you to see that," I tell her, breathing in the clean fragrance of her hair. "I love you, Lacey. I love you."

She lifts her face to me, her smile weak and a little sad, but it's still a smile.

"I love you too," she says quietly. "I still need time. I don't want to rush into anything—not with this job, not with you. But I want to try. I can't imagine losing you over anyone or anything without a fight."

I close my eyes and just hold her close. "It's been a long time since I had anything to fight for."

CHAPTER 25
LACEY

I FEEL his hands reach for me under the sheets. The ceiling fan whirls above our heads, stirring the early morning air. I nudge my ass against Eagle, and he rakes a hand over my bare thigh.

"Mornin', baby." His voice is low in my ears, and I close my eyes just to savor the sound.

He's with me.

Everything is going to be all right.

Mom had book club last night, so we stayed in the sun-room and held hands, talking about work and the status of the construction, while Mom and her friends laughed, played music, and sang inside. I don't even know if they actually read, but they sure have fun.

When we finally put Ruby to bed and went to my room, neither of us slept much. Today's a big day, and even though it's just a formality, I'm nervous. I think Eagle is too. We tossed and turned in bed, tried to make love, watch a movie. But in the end, we just held each other and talked until the wee hours. Now, my eyes are scratchy, but I know there'll be no more sleep for me.

Working with Eagle has changed our relationship. Just like before, he's my sun. I seem to gravitate to wherever he is, pulled toward him by a force more powerful and mysterious than anything I've experienced before.

What's different is Eagle. I never realized how deferential he was to me at the Lantana. He worked for me, so it just seemed normal that he'd follow my lead, ask what I needed. Take instructions and execute them— often without even being asked.

But at Gabriel's Closet, Eagle is a leader. He seems to love project management, and he gets along well with everyone. Our elderly volunteers especially adore him. They all have crushes on "their Eagle," but thankfully, I am a lot more confident that Eagle has room in his heart for only one woman.

Me.

Somehow his having steady work that means something to him has changed us as a couple, too. We talk all the time now. Our conversations are fun, interesting, heated. We argue about work and the construction, and we hope and dream and plan for what comes next. It's been a few months, and Danielle wants to promote me, give me a real paying position, but I've decided to look into opening a consulting firm.

Nonprofits rarely have budgets to pay people big salaries, and I've learned a lot about development. I've hosted parties and dinners, bake sales and food drives, all in the name of raising money for a good cause. It's hard work and exhausting, but there is a need for it. I love feeling like what I do affects people's lives. Not just their dreams, but their reality. And after all, I am really good at planning events. Who says I only need to plan splashy parties?

Maybe I will take the job at Gabriel's eventually. Maybe something else will pan out. I'm okay with uncertainty now. Living in the gray area doesn't mean having no plan and no direction. I prefer to think of it as being open to whatever possibilities may come.

"Lace." Eagle nudges my rear end with an absolutely enormous erection. "Since I don't have to be at work today…"

It's a big day. A formality, but still. Eagle and Linda will appear at the courthouse this morning. The judge assigned to their case will review their petition for dissolution of marriage. If all goes the way the lawyers have planned, Eagle will be absolved of any financial obligation to Linda, and Linda, who's accumulated a truly scary amount of debt in the years she's been married to Eagle, will walk away with nothing more than the problems she created herself.

It's been a dramatic and long road, but today, we all reach the finish line. It's been a tiring race, and I'm ready for it to be done.

"Is it bad that I want to celebrate my divorce before it even happens?" He plants soft kisses along my ear and strokes the back of my neck.

Honestly, I want to celebrate too. A small part of me

is afraid something will stop it. Like a last-second TV drama moment where Linda stands up and declares her love for Eagle. They run across the courtroom, embrace, and live happily ever after.

Even through the worries, I've been trying not to let my imagination run wild the way it used to. Eagle is committed to me. There will be no one to object to the divorce. It's going to happen. We just have a few more hours to wait.

I keep my feet solidly on the ground, at least emotionally, and turn to face him.

"We're still celebrating tonight, right?" I ask.

He nods and reaches between us. We're lying on our sides, facing each other and holding hands.

"Hell yes, we're celebrating tonight. But I already feel lighter, babe. I already somehow feel free. The thing that has weighed me down for two decades is over."

I raise his tattooed hands to my lips and kiss them. Then I slip one of his fingers into my mouth and suck it, running the tip of my tongue over his strong knuckles.

Eagle lets out a low, deep groan. "I wanna wake up to this every day."

I take his wet finger from my mouth and slip his hand under the sheets. I roll onto my back, and he tucks in close beside me. "Me too."

"You think your mom's awake?" he asks.

I look at the watch on my wrist. "She's definitely asleep."

"Then, baby, make all the noise you want." He slides his fingers down my belly and thighs, and I open my legs wide. He lazily traces circles on my pussy, exploring every inch of the tender places he knows so well now.

I turn my face toward him, and he leans down to kiss me. The kiss is soft, gentle, and sweet.

"I could never have done this without you," he whispers.

"This?" I tease, taking his cock in my hand. "Good. Because it's not nearly as much fun alone."

He groans, and I feel his erection jerk in my hand. He slides his damp fingers over my clit, and I sigh, letting him wake me up with long strokes.

His cock throbs against my fingers, and I can't resist him anymore. Lazy touching is fun, but I'm feeling the hot pulses of arousal flood my body with every stroke of his fingers.

"On your back," I tell him, shoving aside the sheet. I get on my knees and crawl over him, then lower my face to his dick.

He does as I ask, a happy grin lighting those blue eyes from deep within. "Whatever you say, boss," he teases, using his old nickname for me. Sometimes we like to play boss-employee. Sometimes I'm in charge, and sometimes he is.

Today, it looks like I get to tell him whatever I want.

"Remember this later today," I say, looking up at him. Then I stroke his balls with my fingertips and draw his cock into my mouth.

"Fuck," he groans, watching as I suck him in, my eyes never leaving his.

I take my time with him, letting my saliva drench his cock, sucking the head so that when I pull my mouth away, my lips make a little pop noise.

Finally, he drops his head back on the pillows. "Babe..."

"You taste so good," I tell him then suck him in so deep, I can feel the head of his cock at the back of my throat. I work his shaft with my hand and his head with my mouth until he fists my hair and stops me.

"Babe," he pants, "you gotta get yours before I get off."

I nod and give his erection a couple of featherlight kisses before I kneel above him. I straddle his lap and rub my pussy lips and clit along his length, just rocking and riding, letting the pressure build. He takes my tits in his hands, his fingers pinching my nipples until I gasp and have to cover my mouth with my hand to quiet the sounds.

Mom's asleep, but she's not comatose. If I scream, she'll definitely hear me.

"Should we get our own place?" I ask, speaking the thought before my brain can stop it from coming out.

Eagle's eyes fly open, his hands still on my breasts.

"Yes," he says without hesitating. "Absolutely fucking yes."

"I've been thinking about it for a few months now," I say, sliding onto his erection. I suck in a huge breath, whimpering happily as he fills me. Then I continue, rocking my hips slightly in time with my words. "You know, nothing too crazy. Space for Ruby to run..."

Eagle's hands are on my hips, and he's gritting his teeth so hard I can see the muscles in his jaw clench. "Babe," he puffs. "We'll have time. Lots of time to…"

I clench my walls around him tightly and then lift myself up a bit, my hands on his shoulders for leverage. Then I slam down hard, thrusting him deep inside me.

"Jesus, baby…"

"Do you think we need one bathroom or two?" I ask, struggling to maintain my train of thought as the pleasure centers itself deep inside me.

"I'll shit in a bucket if that's what it takes," he pants. "Now, Lacey, fuck me."

I do, digging my fingers into his shoulders and leaning forward so he can suck my nipple deep into his mouth. I rock and ride, working my hips in the rhythm that has become so easy, so familiar, and yet never old.

His mouth is like fire on my breast, and I arch deeper, pressing our bodies together until we're so close, nothing on this earth can separate us. It's a feeling I treasure, and when we finally fall over the edge, we fall just like we'll do everything else. Together.

———

We're tangled beneath my bedsheets, our sweaty legs locked together, watching the sun illuminate my bedroom. Our breathing has slowed, and Eagle is tracing the tip of my nose with a finger.

"I got you something," he says. "But I wanted to save it for tonight."

I grin and lift my mouth toward the fingers that are tracing my nose. I pretend to bite him. "No fair," I exclaim. "You tell me that, then make me wait?"

He caresses my chin with a hand. "Well, technically, I got you two things. This divorce is all for you."

I swat his bare chest.

"Eagle. It's as much for you as for me. So, what did you get me, really?"

I already have my own helmet, a new one in a bright cherry red that I wear when we ride. I even have one of the side compartments on the bike where I keep a blanket for impromptu picnics.

"You want it now?" he asks, a sensuous smile covering his face.

"Your call," I say. "I can be patient and wait for tonight. As long as you come home with a divorce, I'll be happy."

He climbs out of bed, and I take a moment to enjoy the view. I never tire of looking at his tattoos, his tight ass, the faded navy-blue eagle. Although I have to admit, I really appreciate that he's covered the name that once adorned his waist.

Now, he's got a very small bike where the name Linda used to be.

He strides to the pile of clothes he threw on my easy chair and pulls a small velvet bag out of one pocket.

My heart catches in my chest. Eagle and I have said we won't talk about the future. I've been so obsessed with weddings and fantasies my whole life, but I don't want him rushing into a proposal. I certainly don't want him rushing down the aisle before the ink is even dry on his divorce from Linda. We haven't talked about when, but we agree someday. Someday is more than soon enough for now.

When he comes back to bed, he hands me the black velvet bag.

I look at him, this man who's changed so much over the time I've known him. He's more than he was before, and there was a time when I thought he was just a fantasy. A tattooed, sexy biker fantasy.

But now, he's mine and I'm his.

The reality of that is better than anything I could have dreamed of.

I take the velvet bag from him and meet his eyes.

"You didn't have to do anything," I tell him. "You know that, right?"

He nods. "Wanted to. Open it."

I unlace the satiny ties that hold the bag closed. Inside is a small gold chain. I pull it out and see there's a gem hanging from the chain. It's a beautiful red heart-shaped ruby.

"I don't know why people want diamonds when they can have something more colorful," he says.

Tears fill my eyes as I hold up my hair and let him fasten the clasp. The heart falls perfectly in the hollow of my throat.

"Thank you," I say. "I wish I had something to give you. I was just planning on a divorce-night blow job."

Eagle laughs, and I lace my fingers through his. "Babe, that's all I ever want. Do that, please."

We kiss again, and before I know it, it's time for us to get out of bed. Eagle showers and changes, then puts on the suit that he brought over last night.

"Not as hot as your tux," I tell him, smoothing the lapels after he's dressed and tied a simple red necktie. He cleans up so nicely, the charcoal-gray suit and black dress shirt he used to wear to the Lantana looking dangerously sexy on his muscled form. "But it'll make Linda regret what she's missing."

"As long as the judge stamps the forms, I'll be happy."

He gives me one last kiss and a playful swat on my ass, then we head to the front door. Mom is making breakfast, and she's got a plate ready for Eagle.

"Your favorite," she says, pouring him a cup of coffee. "PM cinnamon raisin bread."

He takes the plate and mug she's offered and thanks her.

"You nervous?" Mom asks.

"Me or him?" I pour myself a cup of coffee.

Mom throws me a concerned look. "Both of you."

Eagle shakes his head and holds up his hands like he's in cuffs. Then he breaks them apart dramatically and grins. "Almost free," he says. "It's so close I can taste it."

"And you, baby?" she asks, the question directed at me.

I shake my head. "I'm happy. We're both almost free."

Mom comes over to the fridge, where I'm digging

around for the milk. She touches the necklace Eagle gave me. "This is beautiful. Just like you."

"And you." She gives Eagle a big hug, then Mom and I stand together at the front door, waving as he drives away. "This will be my first divorce," Mom says. "First in the family, I mean."

"Hopefully the last as well," I tell her.

Mom wraps her arms around me, squeezes me hard, and then turns on the music. She sings as she cleans up the breakfast dishes, and I can't help but join in. If I ever had reason to sing, dance, and celebrate, this is it.

Around four in the afternoon, I hear the familiar sound of a bike engine. I'm out back with Ruby, reading in the sun-room while Ruby snoozes on the outdoor couch, her head on my lap.

Once I hear the sound, my stomach lurches, and I can hardly control my nerves. This is it. The moment of truth.

I run through the house, leaving Ruby to sleep outside. Mom looks up from the kitchen table where she's tapping into her iPad.

"Go get him, baby," she says. "Your dream man is waiting."

I rush out the front door, but then I slow my steps when I see him. Eagle is standing next to his bike, sunglasses over his eyes. He looks as gorgeous as ever. He must have gone home after court. His suit from this morning is gone, and he's wearing my favorite gray T-shirt, frayed blue jeans, and his leather vest.

I feel every thump of my pulse in my throat, my

heart in my chest as I walk down the sidewalk. In a weird way, it's like I'm walking down the aisle. What waits for me at the end of the broken concrete path isn't marble and fountains, gilded mirrors and bespoke monkey suits.

What waits for me is the man I love. The real, flawed man. Not a dream, not a fantasy. My reality. And I couldn't love him any more.

I watch as he lifts the sunglasses from his face and shoves them on top of his head.

My expression must say everything that's in my heart because Eagle holds up his index finger, then reaches behind him and pulls a document from his back pocket. It's rolled up like a scroll, and he offers it to me. I stop and just look at him.

"It's official," he calls out. "It's over, Lacey. This copy is for you."

It's real. It's finally happened.

He's divorced.

He's free.

I run the last few steps from the sidewalk to the curb and launch myself into his arms. I don't care if I crush the divorce papers. I don't care if I knock him over. I wrap my legs around his waist, making a fool of myself in front of Mom—who I know is watching from the window. And in front of all my neighbors, too, who probably are getting an eyeful as Eagle holds my ass to support my weight.

I touch my nose to his, and he claims my mouth, kissing me hard, his tongue tasting every inch of me.

He tastes sweet, and I kiss him back, tightening my legs and arms around him, claiming him with every ounce of my strength.

We make out like teenagers on the street until, finally, he sets me on my feet. He opens the side compartment—my side compartment—and puts a copy of the paperwork inside.

"Let's ride," he says, grabbing my cherry-red helmet and pulling it over my hair. He adjusts the fit and secures it, even though nothing's changed since the last time I wore it. It's a habit now. A thing he does every time we ride. It's his way of protecting me. Of keeping me safe and showing me that no matter how wild the ride, he'll make sure I reach our destination safely.

I climb behind him and feel almost giddy with excitement. I wrap my arms around his chest, kiss his back, and murmur against his heat. "Where we going?" I ask.

"Sunset," he says.

I know exactly what he means. The afternoon sun is bright as the rays make their way across the sky. We'll go to our favorite park to watch the sun set over the banyan tree. The thing that was so scary, so invasive, is beautiful and perfect in its own way. Just like life.

As he fires up the engine, I touch the heart at my throat. Then, together, Eagle and I ride the open road that leads to our happily ever after.

———

LOOKING FOR YOUR NEXT FAVORITE SERIES?

Join the Gallo siblings as their lives are turned upside down by irresistible chemistry and unexpected love.

Learn more at *menofinked.com/men-of-inked*
or buy direct and save at *chelleblissromance.com*.

Don't Miss Out!

Join my newsletter for exclusive content, special freebies, and so much more. Click here to get on the list or visit **menofinked.com/news**

Do you want to have your very own **SIGNED paperbacks** on your bookshelf? Now you can get them! Tap here to check out or visit **chelleblissromance.com** and stock up on paperbacks, Inked gear, and other book worm merchandise!

Join over 10,000 readers on Facebook in Chelle Bliss Books private reader group and talk books and all things reading. Tap here to come be part of the family or visit **facebook.com/groups/blisshangout**

Want to be the first to know about upcoming sales and new releases? Follow me on Bookbub or visit bookbub. com/authors/chelle-bliss